PROPHET AND LOSS:

Stories of Extreme Beliefs

by

Kenneth Neufeld

"Prophet and Loss: Stories of Extreme Beliefs" by Kenneth Neufeld. ISBN 978-1-947532-61-8 (softcover); 978-1-949756-91-3 (eBook).

Published 2018 by Virtualbookworm.com Publishing Inc., P.O. Box 9949, College Station, TX 77842, US. ©2018, Kenneth Neufeld.

These are all for Mary Jo

ACKNOWLEDGEMENTS

"Prophet and Loss" won *Spinetingler Magazine*'s Canadian Short Story contest in 2005. The story appeared in the magazine and was later included in the *Spinetingler Magazine Short Story Anthology 2005*, K. Robert Einarson, ed. (Spinetingler Press, 2005).

"No Time to Waste: October 21, 1977" was published in a different version under the title "True Father Knows Best" in the *Baltimore City Paper*, August 13-August 19, 1993.

"The Block: October 28, 1977" was published in a different version under the title "The Block" in *Cult Fiction: One Writer's Creative Journey Through an Extreme Religion* by K. Gordon Neufeld (Virtualbookworm.com, 2014).

"The Blessing"was published in a slightly different version under the title "The Marriage of the Lamb" in *ICSA Today*, Vol. 4, No. 2, 2013, and also appeared in *Cult Fiction: One Writer's Creative Journey Through an Extreme Religion* by K. Gordon Neufeld (Virtualbookworm.com, 2014).

"The Work" was published in *The Nashwaak Review*, Volumes 16/17, 2006.

"Let's Get Lost" was published in a different version in *ICSA Today*, Vol 2, No. 1, 2011.

"Fair Game" was published in *ICSA Today*, Vol. 1, No. 2, 2010.

"Fake It 'Til You Make It" was published in *Cult Fiction: One Writer's Creative Journey Through an Extreme Religion* by K. Gordon Neufeld (Virtualbookworm.com, 2014).

"Living Water" was published in a different version in *The Windsor Review*, Vol. 44, No. 2, Fall 2011.

Table of Contents

Prophet and Loss

"HURRY UP, EVA."

The long-haired, bearded young man scolds the woman walking behind him, indicating with a jerk of his head the direction they must go. He is dressed in a plaid shirt and jeans and a denim jacket, and wears a small tan-colored leather knapsack. In one hand he carries a walking stick with which he gestures occasionally. On his feet are yellow hiking-boots with large round serious laces. The woman is also wearing boots like this. The hiking-boots are her only concession to practicality: apart from those, she is wearing an old-fashioned blue calico dress down to her ankles, and a blue and black Gore Tex windbreaker. Her backpack is a shapeless black bag made of some artificial material, attached to her slender frame like a hideous parasite. Her feet touch the ground so tentatively she looks as though at any moment she might walk on the air alone.

The man looks slightly gaunt, but nowhere near as ghostly as his companion. She is finding it difficult to keep up with him, yet he does not look back in her direction except to scold her. When he does, she strives to catch up with him, with a sincere but weak effort which falters as the day goes on.

It is a late spring morning, with patches of snow still visible here and there to the right of them, at the higher elevations. From where they are walking the Rockies are a looming presence to their right, but they are skirting the mountains, neither entering nor retreating from them, but following a parallel path of the man's choosing. From time to time he will stop, a small scowl of concentration on his face, looking first towards the city, which is too far away to be seen save for a brown smudge of smog on the eastern horizon; then looking west, to the towering mountains, with the air of one who owns them. He clutches a modest black leather-

1

bound book in his hands. He seems to be surveying, pondering, waiting.

Whenever he turns to scold the woman, she looks at her feet and answers, "Yes, Jacob." But at one point she glances up at him and asks softly, "Please, could we take a break? I'm so thirsty."

The man regards her with scorn. "Of course you're thirsty. So am I. But we must resist the body if we are to receive the vision. God will not give us the vision until we have fasted for forty days, as Jesus did. God will visit us when we are ready. He will tell us what will be our part in the End Times."

The woman bows her head slightly, accepting. At that moment a shadow passing over them catches their attention. Looking up, they see a pair of eagles swooping low over them before soaring up again into the nearly cloudless sky. They are flying east – perhaps to reach the city.

"It is a sign," the man says, and then opens the book in his hand with a sure touch, quickly finding the right place. "Matthew 24:27-28. 'For as the lightning cometh out of the east, and shineth even unto the west; so shall also the coming of the Son of man be. For wheresoever the carcass is, there will the eagles be gathered together.' These eagles are gathered together to attest that I myself am the return of the Son of Man in the flesh." He continues to follow the path of the eagles with his eyes, as does the woman, who answers, "Yes, Jacob."

❧❧❧

It is almost two years since I met Jacob. He came to a Bible study meeting at our church. I could tell that the other people didn't like him, he seemed so strange. I was the shy one, the one who rarely spoke at the meetings. Jacob came into the group with his long hair and beard and his well-thumbed Bible and from the first time he attended he seemed to dominate the meeting. Even when he was sitting quiet, listening to others, he was the unmistakable focus, the unofficial leader of the group. Naturally the lay pastor who led the group soon took a strong dislike to Jacob. I did not know, when I first laid eyes on him at that Bible study meeting, that only a few months later, in defiance of my parents' wishes, I would promise to Jacob that I would marry him.

⌒⌒⌒⌒

"Let's go, Eva," the man says when the eagles are no longer visible. They resume their quiet pilgrimage, following a fading little-used trail through a scrubby forest. Since there is little water in this area, the trees do not grow as tall as in the more mountainous areas, which are fed by glacier waters.

After about an hour, the man stops, looking down at something near the path. "What is it, Jacob?" the woman wonders as he prods it with his walking stick.

"Cougar scat," he answers, giving her a significant look. "We'll have to keep watch. It's probably somewhere nearby." He opens his Bible and at once finds what he is looking for. "The mountain lion is like those who do not believe, Eva; he will devour you if you have contact with him. Jeremiah 5:6: 'Wherefore a lion out of the forests shall slay them, and a wolf of the evenings shall spoil them, a leopard shall watch over their cities: every one that goeth out shall be torn in pieces: because their transgressions are many, and their backslidings are increased.' The presence of this mountain lion is a sign to you, Eva, to remain faithful and to permit no backsliding."

The woman waits with her head down. "Of course, Jacob," she answers. The man resumes walking, and she follows behind. Soon, they can hear the sound of a small stream trickling nearby. The woman looks up with a revival of hope, saying, "Jacob, I need a drink." He shrugs, looking at her annoyed, but then turns aside from the trail toward the sound. Suddenly he halts. Reaching behind him, he places his hand on the woman's shoulder, and she stops also. He brings one finger up to his lips as she looks at him in wonderment. He points ahead of them, to the bank of the stream, just visible through the trees. The woman cranes her neck forward, and sees what he is indicating: a tawny cougar is drinking from the stream not fifty feet in front of them. The man points back the way they came, again placing his finger to his lips. The woman's face crumples with disappointment, but she complies, following him back the way they came, treading softly so as not to alert the animal.

3

When they are far enough away to feel safe again, the woman speaks. "I wish I could have had a drink. I really need some water, Jacob. Just a little water, nothing more." He looks at her and explodes, "Woman, what am I to do with you? Consider John 4:13-14: 'Whosoever drinketh of this water shall thirst again: But whosoever drinketh of the water that I shall give him shall never thirst; but the water that I shall give him shall be in him a well of water springing up into everlasting life.' Thus spake Jesus to the Samaritan woman. Are you no better than this Samaritan? My words are more refreshing than any water of this Earth."

The woman looks down at her feet, her shoulders slumping slightly. "Yes, Jacob."

It happened this way. Jacob, who had taken to walking with me after all the Bible study meetings, told me that he had received the inspiration that God wanted us to be together. He said that with his special insight into the Word of God, and my humility before the Lord, we could do amazing things together. He said that he had been appointed a special role by God, and that God needed me to help him complete his work. He was just so powerful and assured in him manner, I knew that God must be leading him. In a way he enthralled me from the moment I first saw him. So when he asked me that night to marry him, I told him, "Yes, Jacob. My parents won't like it, but I'm 18 now and I can marry you if I want to. And I will."

The hikers press on until late in the afternoon, when they approach a forestry road that cuts through the landscape like a sword, cleaving it into two halves. The road is fenced with barbed wire running up both sides; farther up, as the road rises to higher elevations, they can see a mountain sheep caught in the fence, bleating pitifully, with its head wedged between the wires. The woman exclaims, "Oh, Jacob, look!" and points to the helpless sheep. The man gives it only a glance.

"The cougar will kill it before long," he comments. At once his Bible is open, and he begins to quote. "Genesis 22:13. 'And Abraham lifted up his eyes, and looked, and behold behind him a ram caught in a thicket by its horns: and Abraham went and took the ram, and offered him up for a burnt offering in the stead of his son.'"

Turning to the woman, he explains, "The sheep represents the offering of your life to God. If you are prepared to give everything, even to die for God's Kingdom which is to come, then God will not require your life, but will take your suffering instead, which will be remembered in the Book of Life. Because you have fasted, and have gone without food and water for many days, God will lift you up, and will grant you a vision of the End Times."

At first Jacob only liked to go camping for the weekends, because we both had jobs and couldn't get away during the week. But after a while more and more people started coming around to our apartment, where Jacob was holding his own Bible study meetings now. He had a way of finding people who were unsure where to go next in life, and convincing them he knew the answer, if only they would listen. And they did: after a few months, we had several young people coming over almost every evening, and a married couple, who let us live with them, so we could save rent and Jacob could focus on his Bible studies and prophecy. Then Jacob began taking us all away to camp in the mountains, where he said we could escape the corrupting influence of the city. Sometimes we would even go away for a full week if people could arrange their vacations to allow it. On these camping trips we would go for hikes to get away from the other people at the campgrounds, and we would find an isolated place by ourselves where we could build a campfire. Beside the fire, Jacob would preach to us for hours. Always, the firelight would flare up to reveal Jacob's lean, intense face, while he read from the Bible and explained what it meant. We all sat before him cross-legged on the ground. At times the flames would leap up to reveal a glistening bead of sweat dripping from his brow, like the tear of an angel poised to bless the parched and ruined earth.

5

❧❧❧

"We have to keep moving," the man declares, turning at once to cross the road by pushing down the barbed wires so the woman can climb over. She struggles to lift her legs high enough to step over. Her dress catches on one of the barbs. Eventually she frees the dress, leaving only a slight tear in the cloth. The man follows after her, easily pushing down on the wire and lifting himself over, then crossing the road to repeat the process at the wire on the other side. Finally they set off again through the scrubby forest. If there is a trail for them to follow, it is scarcely visible now.

Nearing evening, the man and woman come across a small clearing in the forest – a circle where the ground is relatively flat except for a few felled trees and some grass and weeds. The woman slumps down, seating herself on one of the felled tree trunks and slipping out of her backpack. At once she begins to apologize: "Oh, I'm so sorry, Jacob. I'm so thirsty and wish I could have some water. I just need some water, honest. I don't need food. Just a little water, that's all, and I'll be fine." She looks up at him standing over her and seems to be pleading with her eyes. "Please? Could I get some water? I'm sorry I'm so weak. God's strength is not as great in me as it is in you."

The man looks as if he is consulting his backpack and then says, "I don't have any with me. The only water I saw was the stream we passed several hours ago. You don't want me to go back there, do you?"

The woman bows her head in shame. "I'm sorry, Jacob. But I don't think I can go on without some water. I just don't know. I don't know what to do." And suddenly she is weeping, holding her head in her hands.

The man puts his arms akimbo, watching her as she weeps. Eventually he turns and strikes a large boulder twice with his walking stick out of sheer frustration. Nothing happens. Opening his Bible, he reads: "Numbers 20:11. 'And Moses lifted up his hand, and with his rod he struck the rock twice: and the water came out abundantly.' Eva, God has chosen not to fulfill this Scripture in me, though, like Moses, I am leading you towards the Promised Land. You have failed to do what God requires of you,

6

since He has not granted your wish. Is it too much to ask that you go for a few days without food or drink? Have not many prophets done this, and yet *you* are even the Bride of the Redeemer."

The woman offers no reply, but continues to weep softly. Finally the man shrugs, and turns. "All right," he says over his shoulder as he walks back the way he came. "Wait here. Don't move, okay? I'm going back to the stream to get water. I'll bring it as soon as I can. Why don't you just lie down next to that log? You can rest, and God will watch over you."

The woman looks up at him with tremendous gratitude in her eyes. She slowly lowers herself onto the ground next to the log, and then stretches out with her head resting on her arm as she watches the man walking away into the distance.

⁂

One day Jacob came to me excited by a new plan. He said we must go away together, just the two of us, to await the vision of the Lord about the End of Days. I would have to quit my job, because the vision might take many days and my vacation time would not be enough. So I did as he asked, and we came to this campsite near Canmore, in the Kananaskis park, where we fasted and prayed for many days. On the twentieth day, Jacob said we must arise and walk deeper into the wilderness, so the inspiration can reach us more directly. Of course I agreed, thought I was very tired from fasting and could scarcely keep up.

But now at last he has recognized my need for rest, and has honored my wish for a drink of water. As I watch him walking away I think: there he goes, the Holy One, the chosen Lamb of God. What am I next to him? Though I am his bride, I was born to imperfection. My eyes follow his retreating back until he disappears into the trees. I feel the coolness of late spring all around me, yet still I am only able to lie here, neither sleeping nor waking. As I lie here with my eyes half-closed I feel the coolness of a shadow flitting over my face, seeming like an omen or a visitation. When I open my eyes and look up, I see the eagles tumbling and soaring above me. I am filled with the urge to rise and meet them in the air.

7

❦❦❦

Well after dawn the man finds his way into the clearing again, calling, "Eva! Eva? I've brought the water! Eva?" He is hoisting the canteen of water like a trophy at an awards ceremony. When he hears no response he goes over to the woman lying beside the log and shakes her, saying, "Eva? Wake up, I've brought your water." His shaking only causes her head to loll backwards as he moves her shoulder forwards. This startles the man, and he jumps up and looks down at her for a moment in amazement. Then he kneels down beside her and shakes her again more firmly. "Eva! Eva! Wake up!" Her head lolls back and forth with the shaking, yet still there is no response. "What's the matter, Eva? Eva, what's up? Are you dead? You can't be dead!" Then he stands up and looks at her for a long moment. Finally, kneeling down beside her, he closes his eyes and stays for a moment hunched in silent prayer. When he opens his eyes to look again, he senses a shadow falling across his face. Looking upwards, he sees two eagles circling high above him, tumbling and swirling in the air.

A Higher Plane

HE MET THEM WHILE STROLLING near Ghirardelli Square. Pursuing a plan to apply for work at all the newspapers (now that he had completed his journalism degree), Joe had just driven into town the day before on his motorbike after a 3-day road trip and secured a bunk bed at the youth hostel. It was his backpack that alerted them, he later realized; it meant he was a traveler who would be more likely to listen to their appeals. Two young men walked up to him as he headed toward the waterfront. He'd noticed them earlier because they seemed so strange.

In 1976 (apart from those in the military), few young men sported clean-shaven faces and short hair. Yet it wasn't their cleanly groomed appearance that made Joe think they were strange. It was the odd way they moved together as if they were Siamese twins who shared vital organs. They kept turning together to survey the crowds, scanning every face that went by. They both wore circular wire rim glasses that gave them a naïve, wide-eyed look. Both of them were clad in polyester slacks and had shirts buttoned to the very top in spite of the hot weather.

One of them said, "Hi, where're you from?"

"Montana. Just got in." Joe figured he had a little extra time to talk to a couple of oddballs. It was Friday, and he would not start his job search until Monday.

The other guy lit up when he heard these words. "Oh, yeah! I've been there. Yellowstone Park, right?"

"That's down south. I'm from the north. Ever heard of Great Falls? I come from near there."

This left him at a loss, so the other guy spoke up. "So you're on vacation?"

"I'm looking for a job."

9

They grew more and more excited by Joe's words. What was their angle? Joe couldn't make it out. They looked harmless, but they were definitely after something.

"I'm Elijah, and this is Peter," the first guy announced. He seemed to be in charge. He stretched out his hand, so Joe took it uncertainly.

"Joe Sweeney."

"We're part of this community, you know? We do a lot of social work and we love to bring people together. We're called the Creative Community Project. Anyway, we're having a big dinner tonight, and you're welcome to come. There'll be lots of friendly people, and there's a short talk after dinner about our community. It'll be a really nice time."

"And it's free!" the other guy piped up.

"Well, sure, maybe I'll think about it." Joe didn't have any plans, but he wasn't sure he wanted this.

"Here's a card with a map on it. Our house is on Washington Street. Dinner's at six, but it's a good idea to come early. Then you can help out in the kitchen. It's a lot of work making dinner for a hundred people."

"A hundred people? You got that much room?"

Elijah laughed. For the first time he seemed at ease. "It's a big house! I mean, c'mon, Joe! What else are you going to do?"

"Okay, what the hell. I'll be there." Joe suspected there must be something religious about the strange pair – which meant he wasn't all that interested – but he thought it couldn't hurt to check it out anyway. So why did he feel so uneasy? There was nothing he could point to about their appearance or behavior that seemed alarming; but even so, he decided to think it over.

"Great! When you get there, ask for Elijah and Peter. See you tonight!" And with a little wave, they walked on, still scrutinizing the crowds in unison.

In the end, he went, after turning the entire exchange over and over in his mind several times without finding a single clear reason to refuse. When he got there, Joe was treated like a guest of honor. People he never saw before came over and shook his hand enthusiastically. Elijah and Peter sat beside him throughout the dinner, as did two young women from Germany who happened to also be staying at the youth hostel. Dinner was vegetarian lasagna. Joe didn't mind having to sit cross legged on the floor while he ate, since everyone else was doing the same. They were all so friendly that it seemed like no great inconvenience. After dinner members of the Family (that's what they called themselves, "the Family") sang songs and performed skits that all had the same theme: once upon a time, they'd been miserable; now, they were living happily ever after.

Just when Joe thought he couldn't take much more of this, they introduced the speaker for the evening, an attractive woman in her mid twenties with short black hair named Miriam. The main thrust of her talk was that people should keep an open mind and not be "skeptical." She told amusing anecdotes and parables, but when she finally wrapped up her talk, it occurred to Joe that he still didn't know much about the Family. Even so, their enthusiasm and friendliness was infectious. They wanted *so much* for Joe to join them at their weekend workshop on their farm in Mendocino County. The price was only twelve dollars, and a bus would be leaving soon after dinner.

Elijah, Peter and a couple of others pleaded and cajoled. Wouldn't he join them for two days – just two days – to share in the experience of fresh air, friendly faces and new ideas? Joe was about to beg off when Miriam came over.

"Joe, you just have to come to the farm! You'll be our most interesting guest! You're a newspaperman! I bet you could teach us a few things. Everyone will want to talk to you." Joe was flattered to be called a "newspaperman" when all he had was a degree in journalism. With her working on him alongside the others, he began to feel as if he'd be narrow-minded or selfish if he refused to look into it more deeply.

"Oh, all right." Joe had to admit that he really *was* free until Monday. He could almost hear them all sighing with relief. Peter, especially, had been staring at him fixedly for some time. "But I don't need to take your bus. I can ride up on my motorbike."

This threw them into a fresh round of dismay. "Oh, no, you don't have to do that, Joe," Miriam said. "We'll just keep it in the garage until you get back. You'll save gas and then you can concentrate on the workshop."

How could having his bike around affect his concentration? Joe wanted to ask. But by this time it seemed rude to argue such a small point. Joe wanted them to continue approving of him strongly the way they had when he'd first arrived.

Joe was planning to ride his bike back to the youth hostel to pick up his belongings for the weekend, but Elijah insisted on driving him over. The German women needed a ride anyway. They had also promised to go to the farm, but when they got to the hostel, they backed out because one of them wanted to continue on their trip, and Elijah was unable to get them to change their minds. In the end, Joe rode back to Washington Street alone. Elijah, for once, was silent on the drive back.

After locking his bike in the back of their garage, Joe climbed aboard the bus they called the "Elephant Bus" (it had some grey mural on the side that looked vaguely like an elephant) and sat down in an empty seat. He'd been hoping he could stretch out and sleep on the way to the farm. But (of course) Elijah immediately sat down next to him, and then, when everyone was on board, Miriam stepped up and stood beside the driver to make announcements. She was soon joined by Bernard, the guitar player from the evening meal. Everyone was invited to join in another rousing sing-along until they were well past the last exit to Santa Rosa. Joe took note of the road signs: Route 101 to Ukiah.

Eventually the Family members let everyone settle down to take a nap, though some of them continued to whisper to each other the whole way. When the bus swung down a smaller road, Joe popped open one eye and made another mental note: Yorkville, 10 miles, Boonville, 17.

When the bus stopped, he sat up quickly. They were idling in front of a barred metal gate with a "NO TRESPASSING" sign illuminated by the headlights. A young man stepped out into the glare of the headlights and unlocked the gate. He gave a high sign to the driver, and then the bus lurched forward. When the bus stopped again, the lights were flicked on and Bernard started strumming his guitar to awaken everyone. "Wake up, everybody!" he announced. "We've reached the Heavenly Kingdom!"

Some of the Family members giggled at this. Joe just collected his things and got off. He felt grumpy and tired and all he could think about in that moment was how he could get some real sleep.

"Sisters go to the trailer, brothers to the Chicken Palace!" Bernard announced. "Ask the person who brought you to show you the way. And be quiet. Some people are already sleeping."

Elijah practically took Joe by the hand to lead him to the Chicken Palace, which was a ramshackle wooden structure that had once been a large chicken coop. When they entered, Joe found that there were already quite a few other "brothers" stretched out in sleeping bags, so they had to tiptoe through the prone forms to find a space. When at last he found a vacant spot, Joe threw down his bag and climbed straight in.

"Good night," Elijah whispered.

"'Night."

But instead of getting into his own bag, Elijah knelt down and began to pray, with his palms crushing into each other as if this would intensify his prayer.

The next day came before Joe knew it. "Oh, when the red, red robin comes bob-bob-bobbin' along, along!" Bernard crooned, banging open the creaky door and twanging his guitar. He was strolling between the sleepers as the early morning light filtered in. Almost immediately, all the Family members leaped up and began rolling up their sleeping bags. While Bernard continued his song, most of the guests blearily popped their eyes open and a few even sat half ways up.

"Rise and shine, Joe!" Elijah called. With this racket, Joe wasn't going to get any sleep anyway, so he thrashed his way out of his sleeping bag and stood up. A few of the more stubborn guests tried to burrow even deeper into their sleeping bags. Bernard stood over them, crooning as loudly as possible, accompanied by Joshua on the fiddle. That got them up.

There was a long line up for the brother's washroom, so Elijah and Joe stood in line and waited. When Joe's turn came, there really wasn't room for another person, but Elijah stood outside the door and continued talking to him over his shoulder while he waited.

All this togetherness was starting to be overwhelming. Not only did Elijah go with him to the bathroom; he also stood beside Joe during the song fests, sat beside him at every lecture, and walked with him to every group meeting. The lectures were vaguely about idealism, God and goodness, but the lecturer cited psychologists like Maslow instead of quoting Biblical texts. Nearly every moment was either a scheduled activity or a hurried transition to the next scheduled activity, and whenever Joe tried to go off on his own, Elijah followed, insisting he'd get more out of the workshop if he would just set aside his "concepts" and stay with the group. This was turning out to be a lot less relaxing and a lot more lecturing than he'd expected on what was supposed to be a fun weekend. But Joe figured he could put up with it for two days.

When the workshop finally wrapped up on Sunday night, Elijah and Miriam and several others insisted that the only way Joe could truly understand the Family would be to stick around for the full five-day seminar, where they were going to delve more deeply into their teachings. Miriam really went to work on him then, and he was starting to wonder if she was attracted to him. Joe certainly liked her looks. But he had a feeling things just didn't work that way in the Family. They never seemed to size each other up the way other people did, and the sexes always slept in separate quarters at night. Still, when Miriam pleaded and cajoled with him, Joe found it almost impossible to resist. His job search at the *Chronicle* and other papers could stand to wait one more week. They'd said nothing in the lectures that was truly upsetting during the first weekend – in fact, they made God sound like something abstract and universal, the way he was apt to think of Him/Her/It anyway – so Joe agreed to stay on; and when the five days were up, they said, well, why not stay for the weekend when there would be a lot more people around and it's a lot more fun? So, like most of the guests who'd stayed the week, Joe agreed to stay through the second weekend as well, though he'd already heard those lectures.

And then, because he had disputed many of the ideas he'd heard during the five-day seminar (which was a lot more religious in tone and took the Bible much more literally than the weekend seminar), Miriam cajoled and pleaded until he finally consented to stay on for still another five days to hear the same lectures again so

14

he could "*really* understand." Miriam insisted that if he went away without *really* trying to understand, he would be missing a once-in-a-lifetime opportunity to hear a great Truth; whereas, if it turned out not to be the Truth, all Joe would lose is one week. That argument made sense – sort of. But what was it about the Family members when they whispered together? Joe had overheard something about someone they called "Father." Then one of the other guests had taken him aside and told him the Family was connected to the Unification Church, led by the Reverend Sun Myung Moon, but Joe had barely heard of him and didn't know what to think.

Joe was starting to feel more and more divided. On the one hand, he liked how enthusiastic they were about everything, and the way they gave him so much praise for even the smallest acts of helpfulness – for example, if he offered to help make the sandwiches, or set up chairs for the lectures and then took them down again – simple chores they called "actualizing." Joe certainly didn't have any objection to helping out a little; in fact, he liked to pitch in.

On the other hand, the ideas they were teaching him were becoming harder and harder to accept. They claimed, for example, that all of human history since Adam and Eve had consisted of a series of parallel events echoing down the millennia, all pointing to this very moment – the final years of the twentieth century – as the End Time when God would finally accomplish the Kingdom of Heaven on Earth. The lecturer, a slender man named Joshua with a strong but nasal voice, liked to draw a diagram showing how all the years between Adam and Jacob in the Bible paralleled the events from Moses to Jesus; and these events, in turn, coincided neatly with the events of Christianity from the time of Jesus to the present. Their conclusion? "These are the Last Days!" Joshua announced, pounding the blackboard in his excitement. The Family members erupted into applause and shouts of euphoria.

"God tried with Noah. He tried with Jesus. God always succeeds on the third attempt! The Messiah is alive on Earth at this very moment! These are the days when the Messiah must come to bring mankind back to God!" This lecture ended on an incredible high. When the audience broke into smaller groups, the Family members in Joe's group were all brimming with feverish hope. And yet Joe just couldn't quite believe that the correspondences between similar eras in these "Parallels of History" were anything more than a mere coincidence. Surely anyone could find a pattern in history if they played with the numbers enough, he told the group. His comments earned polite applause and glum expressions. Joe felt ashamed for dampening the mood of these bright, friendly people.

More and more, Joe felt as if he were dividing into two selves; one that wanted very much to please the Family members; and the other that found their ideas strange and their conformity stifling. One night, for example, Miriam's group gathered under the stars at the end of a long day and each member softly "shared" his or her hopes and dreams of what the "ideal world" might be like. They were in a tight circle - four men and five women - with their arms interlinked in a "group hug." In that moment, Joe was overcome by a simple, child-like peace. Looking up, he began to dream of a world where all the skies over the entire world were as pristine and sparkling as the skies over that particular farm. When, later, he shared this, his words delighted the group and they applauded, without breaking the hug, by patting each other on the back. When the meeting ended and everyone went to their separate quarters, the feeling Joe had was as warm and magical as the night before Christmas when Joe was five years old.

But the next morning, it was the other Joe - the skeptical one - that awakened. He woke up very early, without the help of guitars and songs. Inexplicably, he was filled with a crushing foreboding - but of what, he didn't know. *Get out!* some inner voice urged. *Get out at once!* He felt he was being pulled into something powerful and incomprehensible that was swiftly turning him into a stranger to himself. Adam and Eve were real people? The Messiah was alive and walking on the Earth? All his ancestors depended on him to be saved?

In his mind, Joe walked through the steps he would have to take if he were actually going to get out of there at once. He would have to get up silently, without awakening Elijah, who was sleeping next to him. He would have to cross the floor of the darkened

Chicken Palace without stumbling over any of the other brothers, and silently open the creaky wooden door. Perhaps they'd think he was just going to the bathroom – but in that case, he'd have to leave all his possessions behind. He would then have to sneak down the long road to the front gate without being noticed, since if anyone saw him, they'd run after him and try to convince him to stay, and yet Joe could come up with no credible explanation for why he needed to leave that very minute. If, somehow, he actually made it to the gate, he'd have to climb over it and go onto the highway to hitch a ride back to Frisco. And then, after that, he'd have to convince the Family members to give him back his bike.

The more he thought about it, the more ridiculous the whole plan seemed. What was he thinking about, anyway – running away in the middle of the night from these friendly people? Abandon all his belongings and sneak out? "Afraid of the Truth," they'd say later. "Couldn't handle the responsibility." Why go to such extremes? Why not just wait until morning and tell them then? So he turned over in my sleeping back and tried to fall back to sleep, squelching the nameless fear that still kept urging him: *Get out! Get out at once!*

Two days later, Joe promised to stay with them forever.

The decision came during the "meditation hour." This was a one hour period during the late afternoon when the guests were permitted to go off on their own to think, pray or write letters. The only requirement was that no one should speak to anyone else. Everyone was to remain alone with his or her thoughts and speak only to God. This was the only unstructured time anyone was permitted all day.

The farm was set in hilly country and had several elevated spots Joe could walk to during that hour. At first, not being in the habit of praying, Joe resisted the whole idea, but finally concluded that no harm could come from trying to pray. After all, if God doesn't answer, he would be none the worse for having tried. And so he tried.

On that particular day, Joe found his way up to his favorite clump of trees. The hilly portions of the lands were mostly barren sheep pasture (though he'd never seen any sheep), and since the climate of the area was dry, there were only a few small patches of trees. But that small clump of trees on the top of a hill was unusual enough to seem appealing. Joe sat down at the base of the trees and began to pray the only way he knew: "Heavenly Father, I don't even know if You're there, but if You are, I really want to find out. I'm trying to decide whether to join the Creative Community Project. They say it's Your will I should join, and I want to do Your will. If You exist, then nothing else matters but to obey You. Please guide me while I figure out what to do. Amen." When he opened his eyes, he was looking straight up into the clear sky, where he could discern a falcon circling over head. When he looked down, he was able to survey the whole valley laid out below.

Joe stared down at the Chicken Palace and the Sister's Trailer parked at the end of the gravel road. His eyes followed the road out to the highway in the distance. There was a barred wooden gate at the entrance to the highway, flanked by orchard trees and a small vegetable garden planted with squash next to a modest house and shed. He knew that one lone brother lived there, with the "mission" to look after the crops.

To his left, there was a small road that wound up a hill towards a wooden structure known as the "Sheep Barn." Seminars were also held at this place. He looked back down to the main area and watched various people walking around, and noticed some activity in the kitchen of the trailer, where they were preparing the evening meal. The late June sun flooded the whole valley with a serene glow, and in that moment Joe could see the farm the way the Family members saw it: everything was idyllic, harmonious – exactly the way God would wish it to be. And, as he gazed out over the valley, Joe pictured himself wadding up all his ambitions to be a journalist into a crumpled ball of paper and tossing it into the waste basket. In that moment, he realized how desperately lonely he was, and how much he longed to accept the friendship the Family was offering him, even at that price. He decided he would.

Joe walked back down the hill to the camp with an anxious feeling in his stomach. It seemed as though the ground was falling out beneath him. Yet he was determined to make this important announcement to Miriam, Elijah and the group.

After he made his announcement, Joe was welcomed by the group, especially by Elijah and Miriam. That night he was the centre of attention. Miriam gave him her own bowl of ice cream as an extra treat, and his whole group was full of good feelings and hope. As they made their way to the Chicken Palace for the song fest before the last lecture of the day, Joe could see only smiling faces of people who were good and powerful and pure in the sight of God. He was especially awed by Miriam, who had been a Family member for four years. Four years! How much God must love her for this, for having served Him for such a long time!

They gathered in the Chicken Palace in a big circle for the usual foot stomping, arm waving, throat wrenching, knock-down, drag-out song session. Miriam went to the front of the room to play the guitar. Sometimes she played with such force she broke strings. They sang Family songs and popular songs (with modified words), but the greatest excitement came, as usual, when Miriam led them through a round of African-American spirituals. Many of the Family members not only sang, they clapped their hands and stamped their feet, and used their arms to act out the lyrics. Today Miriam launched into "Higher Ground," which required a great deal of arm waving.

> "Lord, lift me up, and let me stand;
> By grace, on heaven's tableland;
> A higher plane than I have found,
> Lord, lead me on to higher ground!"

When they came to "a higher plane," they all stretched out their arms and pretended to be airplanes. For once, Joe didn't balk at this silliness; he stretched out his arms along with the rest, closed his eyes, and pictured himself circling over higher ground.

So You Want to Be a Cult Leader!

CONGRATULATIONS! YOU ARE VISITING the Internet's most comprehensive site for career training. You have opted to find out about our online training course, "So You Want to Be a Cult Leader!" Fabulous opportunities are available for those who complete this course and diligently follow its recommendations.

START NOW for only $499! Click here!

In the past, narcissism was often regarded as an undesirable trait; indeed, it was considered a moral handicap that needed to be hidden or dissembled. But in today's world, narcissism is increasingly being recognized as a key marker for personal success. Many people who were mere losers in the past have learned that, by applying the principles of narcissism carefully and effectively every day, they quickly rise to positions of prominence, whether in business, politics, finance, or religion!

Indeed, if you aspire to the ultimate pinnacle of success as a narcissist, you can do no better than to join the ranks of today's most successful cult leaders. Our course will give you a complete list of the skills you will need to found your own starter cult, and then build it up through drawing in more and more followers, until you have grown it into a multi-billion dollar business!

DON'T WAIT! Click here to get started.

Here's a quick overview of this exciting course. So – what does it take to be a cult leader?

LESSON 1: MAINTAIN THE RIGHT ATTITUDE AT ALL TIMES. Begin by repeating to yourself the Narcissist's Creed every day when you first wake up: "Nothing matters except what I want; everyone else exists only to serve me; anyone who opposes me is a loser."

You should repeat these words to yourself wherever you go, whether you are waiting on line, or sitting in the Laundromat watching your clothes dry, or doing any other task. Vividly imagine, as you go through your day, that other people are bowing down to you, or offering up their entire lives to you. Don't permit even one negative thought (such as imagining that other people are your equal or could even outdo you). Our course will teach you how to have an invincible attitude of arrogance at all times, which means you will become unstoppable.

ACT NOW! Click <u>here</u> to get started!

Now that you have the right attitude, your next step is to convert everyone else to the belief that you, and *only* you, matter. You'll be amazed at how quickly you can get others to take this viewpoint also. That's where all the remaining lessons in this course will help you.

LESSON TWO: INVENT AN IMPRESSIVE ORIGIN STORY. Your back story could include such old, reliable favorites as a portentous birth, a precocious and remarkable childhood, or a youth spent acquiring knowledge of business or spiritual matters. Never mind that the origin story is just stuff you made up. You can always accuse those who know the real story of being biased, or deluded, or possessed by Satan, or whatever.

For example, if your cult is based on becoming a success in business, you must claim to be a self-made billionaire and a consummate deal maker, even if you actually started out with a large inheritance, and have gone bankrupt repeatedly. Continue making those claims, all the while maintaining the appearance of success. Eventually, your appearance of success will overshadow any negative stories about you.

You may even want to claim that there were special portents or omens on the occasion of your birth. For example, you can claim that, while you were still in the womb, both your parents individually had dreams that you would grow up to be a savior or redeemer. You can even claim that Jesus or Buddha appeared to you while you were still young to plead with you to be the next avatar. Who checks these stories, anyway? By the time someone shows up to debunk them, your followers will refuse to believe them. Our course will provide you with a detailed flow-chart to help you choose the most impressive and convincing origin story for the type of cult you plan to lead.

ONLY $499 FOR A LIMITED TIME! Click here to get started.

LESSON THREE: ACQUAINT YOURSELF WITH THE ARTS OF MAGIC AND ILLUSION. Those familiar with magic and prestidigitation will recognize what you are doing, but who cares? Your followers will believe that you actually did those things because of your superior powers. For example, you can hide on your person an inexpensive but impressive-looking watch, which you can magically produce whenever you want to bestow a favor on a follower in front of a crowd. With a simple wave of your hand, the watch appears, and you give it to the follower while the crowd goes wild. Who cares if this causes your followers to believe you are God? The point is, it works. Our course will teach you many of the most important tricks and illusions you will need to give your followers the impression you possess divine (or demonic) powers!

DON'T GET LEFT BEHIND! Click here to get started.

LESSON FOUR: TELL YOUR FOLLOWERS THAT YOU ARE THE ONLY RELIABLE SOURCE OF INFORMATION. To become a truly successful cult leader, you will need to convince your followers that everyone else is lying to them, so they must listen only to you. If you do this, no-one can bring any accusation of wrongdoing against you, because once you deny it, your followers will invariably believe you. You could, for example, claim that the news media is "fake" or entirely in the hands of Satan. Similarly, if someone who is considered admirable or noteworthy speaks out against you in public, you can tell your followers that they once were admirable, but now they've fallen under the influence of an evil conspiracy. Our course will teach you all the ways you can get your followers to shut their minds to any outside source of information, however credible, except for those sources that you approve.

WHAT ARE YOU WAITING FOR? Click here to get started.

LESSON FIVE: TAKE COMPLETE CONTROL OF YOUR FOLLOWER'S LOVE RELATIONSHIPS AND SEXUALITY. Your goal as cult leader is to be the only person who really matters to your followers. You must be more important to them even than their own partners. The most effective way to do this is to forbid all sexual relationships or marriage except for those that you have personally approved. But, even after your followers enter into such an approved relationship, you must emphasize that loyalty to you is more important than loyalty to each other. (Of course, any sexual relationship that you enter into with a follower is always approved; indeed, they are required to go along with it.)

But, if doing this seems too drastic or too onerous to manage, you can go to the opposite extreme, and encourage your followers to engage in sexual relationships as frequently as possible with as many partners as possible, (including, of course, yourself). In this way, you have diluted the importance of relationships, so that your followers will feel that their only truly significant relationship is with you.

Either way, you've established with your followers that only you and your wishes matter, even at the price of their marriage or family. Our course will teach you what religious or psychological explanations you should give for why this control of their sexuality is mandatory and why they actually need it for their own good.

SOUNDS EXCITING? Click here to get started!

LESSON SIX: TAKE COMPLETE CONTROL OF YOUR FOLLOWER'S FINANCES AND INCOME. The simplest way to accomplish this goal is to have your followers live with you on a communal property for which you ultimately hold all the deeds and title. In this situation, your followers have no employment or source of income except what you provide them, and, as a bonus, they are insulated from competing sources of information.

But, if you don't feel like running a large commune, you can instruct your followers to live independently at their own expense, which means many will have regular jobs. To counter the outside influences these jobs will have on them, you should frequently ask them to make large donations so you can carry on your work. This will leave them with little, if any, money to spend on other things. You might even make demands so extreme that many of them wind up seriously in debt. If you do this, you've got them where you want them. Our course will teach you the religious, psychological, or practical reasons for why they must live this way and why doing so is ultimately for their own, and for the world's, benefit.

JUST THINK OF THE MONEY YOU'LL MAKE! Click here to get started!

LESSON SEVEN: CONVINCE YOUR FOLLOWERS THAT THEIR LIVES ARE MEANINGLESS WITHOUT YOU. In this final lesson of this amazing course, you will learn how to instill in your followers a sense of their own worthlessness compared to your own magnificence. It actually doesn't matter if your followers are smarter than you are, or better at any given task than you are. Your goal is to convince them that any individual superiority they might have is unimportant – even counterproductive – compared to your own ultimate superiority, which *is something they can never fully comprehend.*

Our course will teach you how to train your followers to believe that, before they met you, they weren't truly alive, anyway. For this reason, you should write inspirational books (or have them ghost written) for your followers. The books could be similar to a book that was published by one of our most successful graduates, which was titled: *One Hundred Deaths You Must Die Before You Live.* Here are some excerpts from this amazing work:

Death Number 1. Lock yourself in a bare room and read only the words of the Supreme Leader, taking no sustenance of any kind, until you expire. In this way, you will purge yourself of all thoughts, news or information you acquired from before the ascension of the Supreme Leader.

Death Number 27. Hurl yourself from a high precipice onto an outcrop of jagged rocks. As you plunge, contemplate the great heights the Supreme Leader commands because of his superb business acumen, and how little you are able to comprehend him by comparison. Die peacefully, thanking the Supreme Leader for his magnificence.

Death Number 42. Leap in front of a tractor-trailer truck on a major highway. In the instant just before impact, reflect how the Supreme Leader's ascension and the total victory of his will is as unstoppable as the tractor-trailer.

Death Number 66. Douse yourself in gasoline and set yourself alight. As your body is consumed, reflect how the brilliance of the Supreme Leader consumes all in its path, and is unquenchable.

Death Number 99. Swallow a slow poison. As you convulse and ultimately die, reflect how the poison of the Fake Media and the liars who pillory the Supreme Leader are poisoning all reason. Die gratefully, knowing that now you are beyond their reach.

DON'T MISS THIS EXCITING OPPORTUNITY! Click <u>here</u> to get started!

Here's an amazing endorsement from a prominent world leader: "After I took this course, I was on fire! I knew that I could do anything I wanted, even though I lack intelligence and skills! By following these principles and applying them to the political realm, I quickly rose to the position of President of a powerful world nation! I highly recommend this course to everyone!"

What are you waiting for? If you follow the tips contained in this fabulous course faithfully, and repeat the Narcissist's Creed every day without fail, you will be amazed how quickly you can become one of the great cult leaders of our time. Anyone can do this, so long as they truly believe in their own importance, and discount the importance of everyone else.

So, are you ready? Let's go! Click <u>here</u> to get started!

No Time to Waste:
October 21, 1977

PUNCHING THE AIR WHILE WE SHOUT out our prayers, we finish morning service. As I jab my own fist forward, I emphasize the words of my prayer at random. My only thought is to show to God my total determination to make my goal for the day—the goal that I pledged in my prayers to achieve for "True Father," the Reverend Sun Myung Moon.

My goal for today is $300. The team captain, sitting in the driver's seat, begins singing "*Uri e so wo-nun tongil,,*" a Korean plea for unity. As soon as I hear this, I end my prayer abruptly. Soon the voices of all eight people in the Dodge van join in the second line, "*Gu medo so wonun tongil.*" We are stopped on a small road overlooking an industrial park on the fringe of West Baltimore. The nearby trees have turned yellow and brown, and there is a trace of a chill in the early morning air.

Immediately after the song ends, Harumi-san, the team mother, turns around from the front passenger seat and gestures for the food cooler to be opened. There is no time to waste. Margaret and Hilda, sitting in the "sisters' seat" behind the driver, lean over to pull out the granola and the peanut butter sandwiches they had prepared the previous night. From the corner of my eye, I watch as Margaret thrusts a spoon into the jar of granola and scoops it into the cardboard bowls, with a little frown of concentration on her freckled face. Margaret is my favorite sister. I'm ashamed of my attraction to her; after all, she is my "sister," and forever will remain so, unless True Father matches us together in some future wedding ceremony. Hastily, I shut down all thoughts of my attraction to her.

The bowls of cereal are handed back to the "brothers' seat," where I am squeezed in beside three other young men behind the two sisters. The brothers bow their heads in silent, five-second prayers of grace, and then bolt down their cereal. There is no time to waste. At any moment, the austere team captain, Reinhard, might point to one of us and give the command to start fundraising. The appointed one would get up at once, grab a box of "product" from the back, and take his cereal and sandwich with him to the industrial park.

This time, however, Reinhard has some news to share, or some announcement to make—or perhaps he is going to deliver one of his reprimands, for which we brace ourselves. He sits sideways in the front seat, eying us piercingly, still holding in his lap the copy of *Divine Principle* he had read to us from during morning service. He sets the book on the dashboard, right next to the glass-covered photograph of True Father. Reverend Moon surveys us from behind the glass, with just a touch of humor and fondness in his eyes—or so it seems to me.

Harumi-san sets a bowl of cereal for Reinhard on the engine hump between them, but Reinhard doesn't touch it. Having served the brothers, the sisters are free to serve themselves. While everyone is eating, Reinhard continues to look us over, sensing whether we are ready to receive what he has to say. Finally, he breaks the silence.

"I spoke with Commander Ishi last night," Reinhard begins. "He said Father is very serious. The Communists are really active, and if it weren't for our members, things would be even worse." He shakes his head at how low America would sink if the Unification Church had not intervened. All of us nod gravely.

"We must all work extra hard during this very serious time," he continues. "Every dollar you collect for Father will help to save America from Communism and immorality. You are very important people. You have a great responsibility."

I feel a lump of peanut butter go down my throat all at once. The responsibility is *too* heavy at times. I cough, and someone hands me a cup of water.

After my throat is settled, Reinhard resumes: "All fundraising regions, nation-wide, must go on a forty-day condition for Father, starting today. This means we will stay out and do a blitz every night, not just on Friday and Saturday nights. People who don't make their goals will have to stay out even later. You must be absolutely determined to bring victory for Father."

The brothers glance nervously at each other, knowing what this means. My chore is to prepare the product every night, so I am often up after midnight and yet still must rise with the others at six o'clock. Even so, I usually reach my goals. Michel, the thin, pale French brother, will struggle for the entire forty days because he isn't strong enough to fundraise vigorously. I hope Reinhard won't put Michel out in front of the 24-hour supermarket all night, as he did the last time we had one of these fundraising conditions. Michel had come back haggard, spaced-out, and depressed, having collected maybe eight dollars and change for an entire night's work. I turned back to Reinhard, who is proclaiming: "We must become the best fundraising region in all of America, to bring honor to Commander Ishi."

"Okay?" Reinhard asks, not waiting for an answer. "So, Mark, this is your area. After you finish that industry down there, I want you to go along the road and do whatever you find—houses, shops—until you get to the main road where there's a 7-Eleven. If you get there early, just fundraise in front of the 7-Eleven. I'll pick you up at noon."

Mark quickly gets up and slides open the side door of the van. He goes around to the back and pulls out a case of product: peanut brittle; two dollars a box, three for five.

"*Mansei!*" Mark shouts—Korean for "Victory forever!"—as he slams the door shut. Immediately, the van takes off for the next area.

❧❧❧

My morning run is a shop-to-shop area along Harford Road, which is dotted with small stores that can be fundraised quickly. In a dog-grooming salon, I find only two people. I breeze in, carting my case of peanut brittle under one arm, and approach the counter.

"May I help you, young man?" the proprietor asks suspiciously, glaring at the cardboard case.

I hold up the peanut brittle, displaying the mouth-watering artwork on the box.

"We're raising donations for Christian youth work," I blurt out before I can get too nervous. "Se we've got this peanut brittle."

The woman shakes her head and says, "No, I can't eat that stuff, I've got diabetes." She parts a curtain behind the counter and shouts into the back room (where, I imagine, someone is combing a cocker spaniel): "Madge! D'you want any peanut brittle?" Back comes the inevitable, "No!"

I thank them, fling "God bless you!" over my shoulder, and race out. There is no time to waste.

The day is progressing reasonably well, with three boxes sold at the auto parts store and another two at the coin-operated car wash, when I enter an imposing music shop on the corner of the next block. The shop is spacious. It has acoustic guitars and other instruments lining the walls, with shelves of sheet music in the back corner. But what especially catches my eye is an elegant grand piano in the middle of the floor. It's a rich mahogany color, and with its lid propped open, it speaks to me with a tonal quality as rich as its color. The sight of it stops me in mid-stride, reminding me of the exams I used to take at the music conservatory.

The examinations were always held on a piano as dauntingly beautiful as this one—no mere half-tuned upright would do!—and there would be an equally daunting examiner, peering at me over her glasses as I made my way to the piano. But then would come the magic moment when the lovely chords rose out of the thing of beauty, and I would be caught up in the pure joy of playing. I always did well. But now that I've joined the Unification Church, I rarely play anymore.

The store clerk, a balding older man with plastic horn-rimmed glasses, comes over to me as I stand there staring at the piano.

"She's a beauty, all right," he says, not even noticing the box under my arm. He sits down on the piano stool and plays a few bars of music, just the first quiet whispers of Beethoven's "Moonlight Sonata." Before the music begin its swelling crescendo, however, he stops, then peers over the rim of his glasses at me with faint amusement, exactly like one of those conservatory examiners. "Do you play, son?"

"Used to," I admit. "I'm out of practice now."

"Want to try? I don't mind, you know."

The man rises to offer me the piano stool, and I walk around and sit down, spell-bound, still holding the case of peanut brittle under my right arm. I lift my left hand tentatively, and play the B minor scale.

"C'mon, set down your load, and give 'er a try," he tells me. The man moves to set my case of candy aside, and this brings me back to the present moment. I look at the peanut brittle, and that's when I remember: there isn't a moment to waste.

"I'm sorry, I can't stay, really," I stammer. "I'm just out today, you know, we're raising funds for our Christian youth group? So we're selling peanut brittle." I hold up a box, trying to recover the determined spirit that had been carrying me along all morning. But it's gone now, rhapsodized away by the brief flurry of notes from the piano.

"I've got dentures, I can't eat that stuff," the man answers coldly. It's as if a door slams inside him. "What group is this for, anyway?" he demands.

No use evading it. "It's for the Unification Church."

"Mr. Moonie? Forget it. I don't want anything to do with that!"

The man turns on his heels and walks away. I get up slowly and heft the case under my arm again, glancing back at the piano as I slip out the door. I've blown it now—I've spaced out. And sure enough, for the rest of my run, the candy is met with indifference, and my religion is questioned and reviled. Waiting for the team captain at the appointed spot, I count my cash: $22, which is $18 short of what I had pledged to make. I would have to repent.

ejejej

Reinhard glances back at me occasionally while I explain. We are driving to the next area. No-one else is in the van except Harumi-san, in her usual spot, so for once I can sit farther forward in the sisters' seat. After my report, I hand in all my cash to Harumi-san, who tucks it away in a small leather bank purse. Reinhard has brought lunch—there are several fast-food take-out bags on the floor—but something in Reinhard's manner warns Harumi-san that this is not the time to dispense lunch.

Soon, we stop on the edge of the parking lot to E. J. Korvette's, a discount department store. I recognize the lot, but I've no idea where it is in relation to anything else in Baltimore. I do know, however, that if I get kicked out of this lot by the store security officers, there are other store parking lots I can work in the same area.

Reinhard is in no hurry to send me off, however. I have confessed my sin of spacing out, and have admitted how much I miss playing piano. Reinhard sees this as a good opportunity to advise me about sacrifice and the importance of having an uncomplaining heart. I listen with a penitent air.

"Sure, playing piano is a fine thing," he says, shrugging. "One day, when the world is restored, you will play for millions of people. But that's the future. You're doing something more important right now.

"God chose you to be a soldier to fight Communism and immorality. You should be so grateful that He chose you for this sacred mission. You know that Holy Song, 'Marching on, Heavenly Soldiers'? That's what you are—a heavenly soldier, fighting a battle for Baltimore, to bring the city back to God! Look around you—who else is listening to God and doing what he asks? We are the only ones. In the future, people who persecute us will come to us to apologize.

"But you know what happens if you complain? All your conditions are lost. All your hard work is wasted. Heavenly Father wants you to have everything, but He can't give it to you, not yet. So if you complain, you break God's heart. And if you complain to me, since I'm your central figure, it's the same as if you were complaining to God. You must stay completely united with me and never complain, if you want to make God happy. Understand?"

I say nothing. Reinhard isn't expecting an answer anyway.

"Good. Okay. So I guess you noticed I went back to the center to get different product. If you want, you can sell pins this afternoon."

I had seen the small velvet boards loaded with costume jewelry when I put away the peanut brittle. I nodded. Pins are much lighter to carry around than boxes of candy.

"Go here," Reinhard tells me, "and if you get kicked out, you can do the Mayco lot across the road. I'll pick you up at four-thirty in either lot. Okay? *Mansei!*"

"Victory forever!" I echo as I jump from the van. I run around and open the back door, selecting a tray of pins. Slamming the door shut, I step back, expecting the van to drive off at once. Instead, Harumi-san leans out her window to beckon to me.

"Robert-san! Here is your lunch!" she calls in her light, musical voice, holding a fast food bag out the window for me.

I run up to retrieve it. Harumi-san beams down at me consolingly, as if to make up for the tongue-lashing I'd just received. I smile back at her and then watch as they drive away.

There is no time to waste. Finding a spot on the curb, I say a 3-second prayer of thanks to God, then devour my lunch: cheeseburger, small fries, milkshake. Refreshed, I straighten the pins on my product board and say a quiet prayer of rededication to my goals. Then I run up to the first person I see and launch into my spiel.

❧❧❧

It's a fine, golden-hot day with just a hint of autumn's freshness in the air. Feeling vigorous, I run from one person to the next all afternoon, striving to recover the strong spirit that will bring with it cold, hard cash for True Father. My method is to run up to the first person I see immediately after I am finished with the last one—even if that person is halfway across the parking lot.

The other rule I follow is that I will only approach people as they are *leaving* the store, not as they are entering; otherwise, there will be complaints to management, and I will be ordered to leave. Luckily, today no-one complains: I enjoy an uninterrupted run, punctuated only by the usual abuse. One person might wave me off angrily, saying, "No way! I don't want any of that junk," but then someone else, six cars away, will look at my pins gleaming in the sun, and delightedly select a yellow Tweetie Bird to give to a child, or a small gold-colored fan for herself. Thanking them and offering God's blessing, I pocket two to five dollars, and then immediately race on to the next person.

In order to maintain concentration, I began to chant in the back of my mind, like a mantra: "Glory to heaven and peace on Earth, victory to True Parents!" I lose track of where I was or what time of day it is as I run from car to car. By the end of the run, I've accumulated $43—exceeding my goal by three dollars!—so when Reinhard drives up beside me, it is a welcome surprise.

This time, Margaret is sitting next to Reinhard in the passenger seat, not Harumi-san. No-one else is in the van. I slide into the unoccupied sisters' seat behind the driver and begin counting out my cash, which I place in the leather purse sitting on the engine hump. I can tell from the way Reinhard hunches over the steering wheel that he is satisfied. I report my results and began rearranging the pins on my display board. "Thank you, captain. Good area!"

"I'm putting you in a house-to-house area with Margaret," Reinhard answers shortly. I feel a guilty twinge of satisfaction at this news.

We are given an area of brick rowhouses near Charles Street. Both of us decide to sell peanut brittle for the evening. We stand together on the street corner as daylight begins to fade, each carrying a cardboard case under one arm, praying for success. After the prayer, I open my eyes first, and look at Margaret's curly black hair twisted around her small ears, with her eyebrows still knitted in prayer, and try not to feel what I can't help feeling.

According to Father's *Divine Principle*, I could commit no greater sin than to seduce her. Even just to imagine kissing her might bring evil spirits that would stop us from achieving our goals. When Margaret looks up and smiles at me, I hastily look away and inspect the surrounding area, as if planning a strategy of attack.

The neighborhood is depressed and poorly lit. If I was fund-raising with a brother, I would suggest working by "O-D-U action," meaning we would each go around the blocks in opposite directions, meeting up again on the other side. But with a sister, this would be risky, since she'd be out of my sight for most of the run. It would be safer if we worked opposite sides of the same street, so I can check on Margaret's progress by simply looking over my shoulder. I tell her the plan, and we set off.

I'm about two-thirds of the way down the block when I hear Margaret calling me. A pleasant tingle runs up and down my spine when I hear her voice—she has a New England accent. I love it. I return to meet her, and we sit down on the curb under a streetlight, holding our boxes on our laps. It's now almost completely night, and in the glow of the streetlight, the road looks cold and deserted.

"I can't keep going, Robert," she says suddenly. "I've got to talk to you. Okay?"

I nod. Part of me is still anxious to keep driving for the goal, but I push this aside and wait for her to say something more. Her small black eyebrows are knitted with anxiety, while she bites her lower lip, which makes me feel even more tenderness. I wish I could just reach out and lightly stroke her forehead or touch her cheek to comfort her—but I must not.

"I wish I could keep going all the time the way you do," she tells me. "I get *so* depressed. But if I talk to Reinhard, he just gives me a big lecture. I've been fundraising for two years now, and it's always the same thing, every day. You know? One time I asked Commander Ishi for a new mission, and he got really mad at me and told me I was a selfish, lazy American. He said Japanese brothers and sisters are working day and night to raise money for America, and they never even get to see Father like I do. He said American members should worker harder than Japanese members. But he doesn't understand—I'm doing my best already, I really *am!*" She breaks off with a sob and bites her lower lip again. I can see that her eyes are watering from tears.

I am aching to reach out and put my arm around her. I imagine gently pressing her small features into my shoulder, letting her tears sink into my shirt and mingle with my sweat. If the *Divine Principle* didn't forbid it, I would be her lover. But instead of touching her, I simply plant the box of peanut brittle more firmly in my lap, waiting for her to say more.

Margaret must have an inkling of my feelings, because she looks at me more directly than before. "I knew you'd understand, Robert. You're different, you know. You really *care* about ... about people." And here she lifts her hand and lets it rest very lightly on my arm.

Two things happen at once. The gentle tingle in my spine now races through my body like a lightning bolt. But just as quickly, an

37

alarm sounds in my head, loudly and insistently, warning me of the danger of pursuing these feelings. If I give in, if I lift my hand to close over hers, we might be tempted to run off together, and then, True Father says, we would have to languish in Hell until Satan himself had repented.

Time stops. I look at her hand on my arm. Maybe if I tell her how I feel about her, this will give her the courage to go on working for Father. But there is no guarantee Father will match us together at the marriage Blessing. If I want to love Margaret, this is the moment. But the idea of leaving True Father terrifies me.

After a moment, I slide my arm out and let her hand drop onto the peanut brittle. She pulls it back then, looking confused and uncertain, and begins to stare down at her sneakers, which are working away at a little pile of dust by the curb. Desperately, I try to shake off all the thoughts that had just raced through my head. I try to think what Reinhard would say. When the words finally come, my voice is oddly tinged with the Germanic speech habits of our "central figure."

"Yeah, I know what you mean," I say. "But these problems are temporary. You think it's going to be this way when the Ideal World comes? Father says that if we do our responsibility, by 1981 all the world will be demanding to hear *Divine Principle*! Many rich people will join, and give everything to Father, so we won't have to fundraise anymore. Just four more years, Margaret! But this will only happen if we work hard and don't complain. God was going to let the Israelites go straight to the Promised Land, but they complained, so He made them wander in the wilderness for forty years! We can't make the same mistake. Do your best, Margaret. That's all God asks. It's just for a few more years, and then it'll be over."

Margaret nods wearily, staring down at her shoes.

"So let's go back to work, okay?" I tell her. "Do you want to say a prayer, or should I?"

Margaret barely glances at me, and then bows her head meekly for prayer. "No, you pray, Robert."

I pray for both of us, quietly at first, but gradually building into another prayer of determination, with half-shouted words accompanied by punching the air with clenched fists. I'm not concerned that an outsider will notice, since the street is deserted. When I finish, we both stand up and walk back to where we'd left off. "See you at the end of the block," I call as I run off.

"Okay," she answers, not glancing back.

❦❦❦

While we wait on Charles Street for the nine o'clock pickup, Margaret remains silent, so I leave her to her thoughts and instead look forward to the night's work. It's Friday, and that means the team will stay out until two or three a.m. to sell flowers to the late-night crowds in bars and restaurants. I find this extra work exhilarating, rather than tiring, because there is usually a good response on these "blitz" runs.

I'm in an optimistic mood when Reinhard comes by with a full van to pick us up. The whole team is reunited, and the storage area at the back is crammed with buckets filled with carnations. Everyone, except Margaret, seems to be in an upbeat mood, and I happily squeeze into the brother's seat next to Mark, who gives me a friendly slap on the back. Harumi-san makes the usual announcement: "Reinhard brought us a special treat – *pizza*!" This is always one of the highlights of Friday night. After counting my cash and turning it all in, I'm handed a slice of Hawaiian pizza.

Margaret tells Reinhard that she hadn't made very much on the last run, so she is going to keep her cash to use as change for the next run. Reinhard nods coldly.

My blitz run – as usual – is the "Peninsula," a long string of small bars and pubs in a working-class area. The first few bars I always go to are located on streets lined with stone rowhouses, and I know exactly where each one is and what kind of welcome I will get. Some of these places kick me out every Friday and Saturday night, but that doesn't stop me from going back the following week. After the first few scattered bars, there are larger establishments where young people dance, and it's in these places that I usually get the most results – if I'm having a good night. On a good night, the young men in the bars see me merely as a provider of carnations, which in turn are an easy way to please their girlfriends, so I might collect as much as $200 on one four-hour run. On a bad night, these same young men will look at me and

39

know I'm a hated "Moonie," and they will abuse me verbally and order me to leave.

I pray urgently to have a good night, but steel myself for the worst.

☙〜☙〜☙

It *has* been a good night, and my bucket is almost empty. I'm standing on a street corner, holding my few remaining carnations in the hope of making one last sale for Father. My pickup time was supposed to be 2:30 a.m., but it's now nearly 3:15. This is not the first time Reinhard has been late. There's nothing to do but try to sell out my bucket. A man who walks by becomes furious when I approach him with my carnations at three in the morning.

"Go home!" he orders, like a child scolding a pesky dog.

But I have no idea where I am, and in any case, it is my duty to wait until my central figure comes for me. I wait.

Finally, the Dodge van appears at quarter to four. Probably Reinhard had mechanical trouble, I think. With weary relief, I slide open the side door and sit in the brothers' seat. It's then that I realize why Reinhard is late. Margaret is gone.

"Thank you, captain. Good area!" I report, as usual, bowing my head for a quick prayer. As I hand my money forward to Harumi-san, I dare to ask: "Margaret's back at the center? Not feeling well?"

The dismayed looks everyone gives me make my stomach churn. Did something happen to Margaret? I can't bear to ask. The year before, a young French sister in New York City had been raped and murdered while fundraising. Filled with fear, I wait for Reinhard's reply.

Reinhard turns onto the expressway and drives silently for some time. There is a dull strain of tension in the air. Nobody jokes, nobody tells an inspiring testimony. The pale yellow wash of the streetlights sweeps repeatedly over the seven faces in the van: first, Reinhard and Harumi-san; then Hilda; then the brothers. Everyone is thoughtful, or praying, or staring out the windows at the lowering landscape. When he finally speaks, Reinhard looks up at us in the rear-view mirror. Our eyes connect in the glass. His

40

eyes are as gray and cold as I've ever seen them, and his words are flat and toneless.

"Margaret wasn't at her pick-up point," he says. "I asked inside the restaurant where she starts her run, and they said she asked for directions to the bus depot. She told them she was going back to her family in Boston. She gave them her flowers, and left. When I got to the depot, the bus was already gone."

So that was it. Margaret had left. She'd joined the ranks of the unbelievers – the walking dead. To keep Reinhard from seeing the tears in my eyes, I lift up my hands and begin to pray aloud, and soon all the others join in, and it becomes a unison prayer of repentance. Margaret had left; the team must have set a bad condition.

As the crescendo of our prayers grows louder, my mind rages with the fear that it was really my fault that Margaret left. If I had responded differently to her touch, would she still be here? Then an even more dangerous thought occurs to me: perhaps I should go after her. But how could I? Then I remember that my brother lives in Boston. Would he help me find her? But I don't dare leave Father. If I do, I will die.

Yet, even as these thoughts are raging through the back of my mind, the prayers I speak aloud are much like the prayers of everyone else on the team. I pray that Margaret will realize her mistake and come back to the True Family. I promise to God that I will work even harder as a heavenly soldier for Father. And then I turn my thoughts to preparing the product for the next day.

There is no time to waste.

The Block:
October 28, 1977

"SATAN IS COUCHING AT YOUR DOOR, and his desire is for you," Reinhard tells me, jabbing an accusing finger in my direction. He leans around from the driver's seat of the van and glares back at me. The garish pink light of a neon sign is all that illuminates his ski-jump nose and long, mournful Austrian features.

I know Reinhard is quoting to me from the Bible, though I have never read it. Chances are, he hasn't read it either. The words he is reciting are words that we have both heard in lecture after lecture of Reverend Moon's *Divine Principle*.

I had just told him I wanted to keep all the money I had made earlier to use as change for my customers on the blitz run. Does he suspect my plan – the plan I keep trying to push out of my mind? The plan I might, or might not, do?

My legs tense as I crouch in the seat behind him, clutching my bucket of carnations, ready to leap out and start fundraising the instant he gives the command. We are the only members of the team still left in the van. I know why he is putting me here. Earlier, Reinhard had dropped Mark off to sell flowers in the pubs in the Peninsula--which was where he usually puts me for the late night blitz run. Now, we are parked on The Block, somewhere in the centre of Baltimore.

"You know what this place is, don't you?" Reinhard continues. "This is Satan's domain. Satan is in charge here." He gestures towards the street in front of us: one solid block of peep shows, porn magazine shops and sleazy bars. One solid block of Hell.

"Of course, Satan controls *everyone* outside the Unification Church. Even our parents." Reinhard is merely repeating familiar phrases, but soon the lecture will get more personal. I relax slightly. It will be a while before he orders me out. I await his onslaught.

"But Satan doesn't always get his way with other people. Here, he does. Fornication, lust, perversion. Anything he wants." There is a black-covered hardbound edition of the *Divine Principle* on the engine hump next to Reinhard. Beside it, the face of True Father, Reverend Sun Myung Moon, stares at me accusingly from a gold-bordered frame. Reinhard opens the book to Chapter Two.

"Of course you know why Satan is so powerful. As the archangel Lucifer, he seduced Eve and they fell. Then Eve seduced Adam and he fell, too. Now whenever anyone--except Blessed Family members--has a sexual relationship, they are repeating the original sin, and it makes them even more of a child of Satan." Reinhard shows me the title to Chapter Two: "Fall of Man," then closes the book with a bang.

"I know you had a Chapter Two problem with Margaret." He raises his hand when I start to protest. "I'm not saying you fell. I just mean you desired her. You had lustful feelings for her. You were guilty of the fallen nature of leaving your proper position. Because of this, you made a condition so that Satan could invade and take her away."

His words are a slap to my face. Of all the team members, I was the most upset when Margaret left. Now, a week has gone by, and the others no longer mention her name. But every night, I pray she will come back, though I'm not sure if the reason I want her back is for True Father, or for me.

And yet, there is no answer I can give to Reinhard. As the team captain, he represents the Messiah. He must be obeyed at all costs. If I don't obey him, it would be un-Principled, and Satan would have a condition to invade me also. And (as I have been told many times), if Satan takes me away from the True Family, I will probably go insane or commit suicide or have a fatal accident. All I can do was listen in silence, and try to unite with Reinhard's words.

"You must forget about Margaret now, and think only of True Father," Reinhard says urgently. "Margaret is dead. At least, she is dead to Father, which is the same thing. I knew something was wrong with her, even before she left. Remember how she used to blitz the pubs on Eastern Avenue, and bring back $300 every time? People thought she was such a heavenly sister, really dedicated to Father. But once she told me, 'I'm just using God!' She thought there was something *wrong* with bringing so much money to Father. She wasn't seeing from God's viewpoint. So Satan could invade. Okay! I'm not going to talk about Margaret any more. Forget her."

Reinhard points out the windshield at the brightly-lit street ahead. "You must go out and battle Satan directly, to restore your fallen nature in the sight of God. You must take dominion of this area and bring as much money to Father as if you were back in the Peninsula. Stay centered and think only of True Father and the Principle. Okay? *Mansei!*"

This Korean word--meaning "Victory forever!"--is the signal to start fundraising. At once, I stand up and repeat, "*Mansei!*" I slide open the side door and leap from the van. Pushing the door shut, I stand back and watch as Reinhard immediately pulls away from the curb.

I am on The Block.

☙☜☞☙

Finding a quiet, darkened doorway on a side street, I set down my bucket of flowers and began a prayer of dedication to start my run. I ask Heavenly Father to help me find the courage to "crush Satan" and claim the area for True Father. I pledge my determination to "break through" the evil spiritual world surrounding the area so that God can touch these people's lives. Even if they only make a small cash donation to Father, or buy one of his flowers, God will have a "condition" to raise them up spiritually. I pray that God will accept each purchase as an offering, and bless the people accordingly. And, finally, I repent for thinking so much about Margaret. For one last time, I ask God to take care of her, wherever she is, because I still love her. And then I vow to think of her no longer, but only of Father and my mission. In order to seal my pledge, I take note of the date, so that I can make a new start. It is October 28, 1977.

As I start my run, I try to figure out the best way to work the area. The street is busy, with cars stopping and starting and many men going in and out of various places. They are all in too much

45

hurry to look at carnations. I get the usual wisecracks. "Who died?" laughs an older man going by, while another, in a similar vein, snarls, "Hell, no. I ain't dead yet."

Stopping people on the sidewalk leaves me weak and disoriented; my determination is dwindling. Above all, my duty as a fundraiser for Father is to keep going, never sit down, and never give up. I look for a way to regain momentum. I decide to treat The Block like I would a shop-to-shop area. I will go into each place and sell to anyone I encounter. This presents a great challenge. I will have to do a lot of seeing-without-seeing: my eyes carefully looking only at the people I speak to, while avoiding looking at the pictures on the walls or on the covers of magazines. If the images can't be avoided, I will have to let them glance off my retinas and fly away. But if I don't--if I pause even for a moment too long over a picture of a naked woman--Satan will invade me, filling me with lust and temptation.

To seal myself off as much as possible from the Satanic images around me, I begin a chant in my mind, over and over again, like a mantra: "Glory to Heaven and peace on Earth, victory to Father, smash out Satan." And then I go to work, stepping into the glaring fluorescence of a porn shop. The walls are lined on both sides with magazine racks. I look down at the floor until I reached the counter. The counter itself is a bacchanalia of phalluses and gadgets whose purposes I don't even want to imagine. I stare into the eyes of a bored-looking man behind the counter. He is very pale, with short blonde hair, wearing a red T-shirt. On one of his arms is a tattoo: a cross with chains around it. He is reading a motorcycle magazine. The magazine's cover depicts a woman clad only in a black leather jacket, straddling a Harley. I try not to look at the cover, but only at him. The effort of not looking is almost unbearable. I feel the raw strain of tension in my chest. *I have not touched a woman for more than a year*, I think, then immediately reject this thought. *Glory to Heaven. Smash out Satan.*

At last the man looks up glumly when he notices me standing there, not saying anything. "Yeah?" he tosses in my direction.

"We're selling carnations for our Christian youth program," I tell him, lifting up the bucket. The pink and white heads of the flowers bob up and down hopefully on their stems.

"Nah. Don't need any. Thanks." He returns to his magazine. I leave, stopping only to accost someone by the magazine racks. He waves me off impatiently without a word. With enormous relief, I return to the street again. The next door down is the entrance to a stripper bar. I step into the dimly-lit lobby, and when my eyes adjust, I can see a heavy-set woman behind a glass window to the ticket booth, collecting the cover charge. The bar is hidden behind two black curtains drawn over the entrance. Her hair is pushed up high, a reddish color, and she is wearing an imitation pearl necklace. I sense her attitude is friendly.

"What ya got there, son?" she asks, looking down at my flowers. "Oh, ain't they pretty!"

"I'm selling flowers for my Christian youth program," I mumble, but she isn't really listening. I can tell she wants to buy.

"How much?"

"A dollar each."

The woman pulls out a dollar and asks for a pink one. As I give it to her, I ask if I can go into the bar to sell to the customers, but she shakes her head. "Sorry. Boss would have a fit. You can stand outside and ask 'em if you want." I thank her and left. I have to keep going.

The next store down was another porn magazine shop. The smell of these shops is unforgettable; they all have the same cloying-sweet odor that hangs in the air like a shroud. Whenever I walk into that atmosphere, I feel as though I'm burrowing into a human body, becoming one of its secretions; it is very dense and physical. As I make my way to the counter, I again have a wrenching feeling from trying not to see the pictures that are everywhere at hand.

"Sorry, buddy," the man at the counter says before I even open my mouth. "I had a guy here last week, told him the same thing. We don't have much call for flowers. Thanks anyway." He's not unfriendly, but there is no point hanging around. I quickly thank him and start to leave.

As I turn to go, however, my glance is caught squarely by the sight of a magazine cover depicting a woman, looking back over her shoulder. She isn't wearing anything. The sight is like a blow to my face, stopping all thought for a moment. Even the chanting ends. I catch my breath and quickly exit, knowing the picture has impressed itself on my mind in spite of my efforts to block it out. It calls out to me from across the gulf to another world, a world I am trying to lock away: the world from "before the Family." I am shocked to see how much I'm still attracted to that world, even though I have been taught to fear and despise it.

Now I've done it, I think, running out onto the sidewalk and looking for a place to pray. Memories press upon me of a world I thought was behind me forever.

❧❧❧

Part way down The Block, there's a break in the storefronts, leading onto a side street. I determine to go down that side street, find a quiet spot, and pray fervently, in an effort to drive away the evil spirits swirling around me. Breaking into a run, I reach the side street in a few strides. It's really just an alley, poorly-lit compared to the gaudy neon glare of The Block.

A young woman is smoking a cigarette as she leans against the wall of a building half-way down the alley. She has on a short skirt and high white leather boots that come up to her mid-calves. The boots and her knees glint with a dull allure in the dim half-light.

I turn my back on her, set my bucket on the ground, and resume my chant. Aloud. *Glory to Heaven and Peace on Earth. Victory to Father. Smash out Satan.* As I say each word, I emphasize it by thrusting one fist forward in front of me, as if I'm sparring with Satan. First, a right jab, then a left. *Smash out Satan. Smash out Satan.* I don't even hear her approaching me until suddenly I feel her fingers on my elbow, stopping me in mid-spar.

"Somethin' the matter, Mac?" the hooker says to me, leaning around to peer into my face with part concern and part amusement. Her face is heavily made up, and now that I can see her closely, she looks older than she seemed from the distance. "Oh, look at them flowers!" she exclaims, catching sight of my bucket. "You sellin' these?" She picks some of them up and holds them to her nose. I am still tongue-tied, a bit afraid of her, afraid of the power of Satan working through her. But at the same time, I can see she that she is just like most women I meet. Flowers delight her, and she can't resist smelling them.

48

"Yes, I am," I manage to get out at last. "It's for my church. A dollar each."

She holds up a white carnation on its long, thin stem and turns on a wheedling smile. "Give me one? C'mon, you can give me *one*. A pretty flower for a pretty lady."

I want to tell her no, that she must not take that flower, it belongs to the Messiah. If she takes it without paying for it, it might set a bad condition and she might have to "pay indemnity," meaning she would suffer in some way. Perhaps one of her customers would even hurt her. But I can't get the words out, because it would sound so strange, and she wouldn't understand. She lays the carnation across her gauzy black blouse, as if to show how pretty it would look if she pinned it there, and gives me such a pleading look that finally I just nod quickly. Not only will she have to pay indemnity for this; I will, also--because I know the Truth, so God holds me even more responsible.

She breaks the stem off and rummages in her purse for a straight pin. "You wanta pin it on? Be careful, now. Don't poke me." Finding a pin, she holds it, and the flower, out to me.

I raise both hands and shake my head. "I can't do that. It's--it's my church. They won't let us. It's against God's will."

She gives me a queer look and then quickly pins the flower on herself. "What is? Touch a lady? I seen a few reverends in my work and they had no problem." She laughs, a little coarsely. "No, sir. No problem at *all*." Then she becomes more serious and looks at me more closely.

"What church is this again?"

"Unification Church." This usually brings a negative reaction.

The hooker gives me a blank look. "Oh, yeah. Unitarian."

"No, Unification. You know, Reverend Moon. People call us the 'Moonies.'"

"Oh, you're a Moonie?" She takes a step back and looks me all over. She has the same amused and puzzled look. "Don't they make you run around all day sellin' stuff for no pay? What d'you wanta do that for?"

I become more and more afraid as I speak to her. Every minute away from prayer or fundraising increases the chance that I will become invaded by Satan. And especially, to have give-and-take with a *prostitute*! But then I remember that Jesus had prostitutes as followers, and I am seized with the reckless hope that I can win her for True Father. Then, everything would be forgiven, even the flower I gave away. I plunge in.

"I do it because we're building the Kingdom of Heaven on Earth. All the sin in the world is because people don't have the truth. Now Reverend Moon is bringing the truth, and we have to tell as many people as possible. If we don't work hard enough, Satan will invade and Communism will take over. That's why we work all the time. I'm proud to do it." I rattle all this off in a hurry, all the standard phrases that I repeat every night in my prayers, or hear over and over in morning service, all taken from True Father's speeches and *Divine Principle*.

"You don't look so proud to me. Man, you just look beat! That's a funny way to get to Heaven. Wearin' people out like that. Let me ask you somethin.' You got a girlfriend? When was the last time you got to love a lady?"

I can't look at her. I look down at my feet, at the bucket of carnations, their colors washed out by the pale streetlights. Most of all, I'm trying not to think about Margaret. Her freckled face, her small stature, her shy, quick smile. *I never touched her. Not even that one time, last week, when she wanted me to.* But I summon my determination, and I say instead, "We don't believe in that. I mean, not yet. When Father--Reverend Moon--matches me to one of the sisters in the church, then I can do that. Until then, I have to work for God, and think of nothing else."

"You mean you haven't touched a lady in a long time? I bet you'd like to, wouldn't you? You probably got enough money to let me show you a good time. How 'bout it, huh?" She leans closer to me, and peers up at my face.

She guessed right. I have more than enough money for a quick encounter, if we go down the alley into a dark corner. I want to pretend she is Margaret. I want to hold her like I would hold Margaret. I reach into my pocket to touch the small wad of bills, mostly from earlier in the evening.

She sees my hesitation. "C'mon," she says softly, putting a hand on my shoulder and jerking her head toward the darker part of the alley. "Nobody'll know. God won't mind."

50

I finger the bills in my pocket again slowly, and stoop to pick up the bucket of carnations with one hand. Reinhard's face comes into my mind, his finger pointing accusingly at me. "Satan is couching at your door, and his desire is for you." I could never face Reinhard again if I went down the alley with her. I would have to leave the Family and go home. My life would become empty and worthless. God would turn His back on me. Or ... would He?

Suddenly, I have an vision of myself running down endless alleyways and into infinite stores, forever babbling out my sales lines to person after person, for years and years on end. Never knowing one touch from a woman.

And in the next moment my wild plan to look for Margaret comes rushing back. What's her last name, Anderson? I imagined trying to find Margaret by calling all the Andersons in the Boston phone book. Even if I did manage to find her, she'd probably think I was trying to get her to go back to the church. She might say, "Robert, I can't talk to you. I'm not with that church anymore." Or ... would she?

I start running out of the alley, back onto The Block. The woman laughs at me from behind my back: a loud, scornful laugh. "Go get 'em, Mac! Go sell them flowers!" she jeers, but I don't turn. Until that moment, I thought I was better than her, because I was the servant of the Messiah. Now, I know we're both the same: trapped, lonely, and desperate, each in our different ways. I count the bills in my pocket again, including the ones I'd held back from earlier in the day.

There is enough. But I will need to get to the bus station right away. I will go to Boston and call my brother.

Then I will find Margaret.

The Blessing

THERE MUST BE SOME SORT OF DELAY. Already, it's twenty minutes past the time the Blessing was supposed to begin, yet still Sally and Kurt are waiting outside the arena. Sally perspires from the early summer heat.

A double column of brides and grooms snakes down the circular corridor surrounding the main arena of Madison Square Garden. From where she is standing, Sally can't see the end of the line. She knows there is another double column of couples waiting to enter from the other direction. When the doors are finally opened, the two columns will merge into one for the wedding march.

The rumor being whispered up and down the lines is that the delay is because there are security guards with metal detectors at every entrance making sure no-one enters the arena with the intention of killing True Father, the Reverend Sun Myung Moon.

Sally tugs at her veil and the white wedding gown she had made--a Simplicity Pattern (with the neckline raised two inches) that all the brides had used. She knows Kurt is giving her that peculiar look that makes her so uncomfortable.

They had met two days before. At the Matching in the ballroom of the New Yorker Hotel (now called the World Mission Center) just two blocks away, True Father had paired her up with Kurt. This was not the first time Sally had seen the Messiah in person; but on every other occasion, she'd been seated on the floor of a large room listening while Father spoke at length. This time, however -- for one brief moment -- she'd stood right next to Father while he surveyed the room to find a suitable match for her. All the eligible brothers were seated cross-legged on the floor on the right side of the room, while all the available sisters were assembled to the left. Father had pointed first at her. She stood up and approached him. Father then surveyed the brothers for a minute before stabbing his finger in the direction of Kurt, a burly older American brother whom Sally had never seen. She was still jet-lagged from a flight out of England which had brought her to New York the previous day. During the entire flight, she'd been excited but nervous about who would be chosen for her husband.

Remembering her first glimpse of Kurt rising to meet her at the front of the Grand Ballroom, Sally risks a glance at him now. He responds with a nervous smile, momentarily erasing the hungry, almost predatory look he usually gave her. He is a large man dressed in a navy blue two-piece suit, with black shoes, white shirt and white gloves, set off by a maroon necktie of the exact same shade that all the grooms are wearing. Kurt pulls the tie out from his vest and twists it around so she can read the words embroidered on the cloth loop at the back. "World Peace Through Ideal Family," it proclaims, with the first two words in script and the rest (on the line below) in block capitals: "JULY 1, 1982."

"Very nice," Sally assures him, then turns away again to look straight ahead. There is still no movement in the long queues waiting outside the arena doors. Since Father is inspired by God, there must be some reason why God wants her to marry this older man who makes her feel so uneasy. After they were matched, they had gone to a side balcony to discuss the match. Many other prospective couples were already there, but they'd found a small table where they could sit by themselves to talk. Sally could have refused Kurt, but she'd been instructed to trust Father's decision, so she resolved to accept him. Yet even at their first brief meeting, he'd surprised her by admitting he often hid from church leaders whenever he wanted to avoid church activities.

At last, the long line of couples begins moving forward. Well up the corridor, Sally sees that the arena doors are finally open. The two double columns unite at the entrance, forming a single phalanx of eight couples arrayed in alternating colors – blue, white, blue, white – all moving together like a swelling river of humanity flowing into the arena. Now Sally is at the entrance, and the vast space opens up before her, brightly lit, with the floor carpeted in dazzling white. Immediately after entering, the couples climb several steps to a dais carpeted in deep red. They cross the dais, marching in procession, and then descend to the arena floor. Father and Mother, wearing flowing white robes with gold brocade and white crowns tinged with gold, stand on raised platforms on each side, holding large white wands. Beside them are huge bowls filled with Holy Water. Kurt and Sally are the furthest to the right of the eight couples in their rank, and as they pass directly underneath True Father, Sally feels the Holy Water splashing the side of her veil.

As they step down onto the arena floor, the phalanx divides again in two, with couples streaming to the left and right toward their assigned places. Sally knows that she and Kurt are expected to take their places in the bleachers at the back. The arena floor is already completely jammed with prospective brides and grooms. After they reach their spot, Sally and Kurt turn to face the dais where the True Parents are standing in front of two elegant chairs upholstered in red and gold. Father begins the ceremony with a prayer, which booms out over the entire arena in guttural, emphatic Korean, imploring God's presence at the ceremony.

Sally takes a sidelong glance at Kurt. The man she is to marry is a mechanic at the church warehouse in Queens. He fixes the Dodge and Ford vans for the mobile fundraising teams that fan out all over the country, selling flowers and candy to save America. Sometimes Kurt works on the delivery trucks that bring Father's *News World* newspaper to newsstands all over New York. This is important work, but Sally worries about the way Kurt talks about the brothers he works with. No matter whom he mentions, he always has to show he knows better. Even worse is the way he sometimes talks about the sisters. It's as though he thinks sisters only exist to serve the brothers. When Sally told him about her education, he'd dismissed it as merely "intellectual" and "not useful to Father."

True Father's voice breaks into Sally's reveries; he is asking the couples to assent to the four vows of the Unification Church Blessing. He will ask four questions, to which the brides and grooms must shout in unison their assent. He will ask the questions in Korean, but both Sally and Kurt have seen them written down in English.

"Do you pledge to keep the heavenly law as original men and women, and should you fail, pledge to take responsibility for that?"

Kurt joins in the general shout of "Yes!" to Father's question. Sally, however, only sighs out the word, half-heartedly, though Kurt is too caught up to notice.

The marriage Blessing had always seemed like it would be the answer to all her troubles. Over and over, Sally had been told that once she received the Holy Wine at the ceremony following the Matching, she would be spiritually changed. The Holy Wine Ceremony had removed her Original Sin. But Sally hadn't noticed any change since she took the Holy Wine. She remained as she'd always been: often discouraged and prone to depression. She'd hoped that the Blessing would completely free her from the evil spirits that tried to discourage her or take her away from the true path.

When she first joined the Unification Church, the Blessing -- which she'd only learned about after she'd been a member for a couple of months -- seemed like the perfect answer to the troubles that had dogged her all her life. She had never known how to be comfortable around men and had never been in a long-term relationship with anyone. She was taught that Father would find just the right brother to be her soul mate. With his perfect insight into the spirit world, he would find someone with just the right ancestors to match with hers, and together their blood lineages would be removed from the dominion of Satan. So why did she feel so miserable?

Father's voice breaks into her thoughts and Sally turns her attention to the front of the arena. He is intoning the second vow. Sally recalls the English translation: "Do you pledge as ideal husbands and wives to establish eternal families, with which God can be happy?"

"Yes!" everyone shouts out in unison, louder than before – except Sally, who can only manage a half-hearted mumble.

Kurt thrusts out his right arm and clenches his hand into a fist, pumping it for emphasis as he yells out his "Yes!" The brothers and sisters unite in their desire to please Father by pouring every effort into the shouting of their vows.

But hadn't there been one boy, once, back in college? She'd met him in her third year of reading English at University of Leicester. She'd been the quiet one who always sat at the back of the lecture hall. This young man had been in her Restoration Drama course. And now here he was again, seated nearby while her professor talked about Wordsworth.

His name was Malcolm. He looked at her many times without saying anything, but one day he approached her after class. It was clear he was just as shy as Sally. They went out a few times (the first time they just went to Wimpy's for hamburgers), but Malcolm had never known how to put aside his own awkwardness around her. Eventually he stopped trying. Sally went back to believing that she was too plain and ordinary for any man to want her.

Then she'd met the Unification Church, just a few months before graduating from Leicester. She'd been on the way to the chemist's shop for some soap and other things, when she chanced across a young German man and a young Japanese woman standing on the street corner. They were selling a small newspaper called the *New Hope News* for 10 pence, and since they were so friendly (though the woman spoke hardly any English) Sally bought one of their papers. Manfred told her about a meeting of young people at a nearby house, and invited her. He was so impressed with her university education and so flattering that she almost laughed. But she told him she would come, and then she almost hadn't, thinking she would be out of place. At the meeting she'd met a few English men and women, as well as a French man, an Italian, three Germans, and a Canadian. All of them had welcomed her and exclaimed about how smart she was to have progressed so far in her studies. There was one other guest, a young woman who worked as an *au pair*, who'd met the *New Hope News* sellers while pushing her young charges in a pram. But the *au pair* woman never returned.

Sally came back several times. The church members gave curious lectures about God and Jesus that made her think. But it was really their friendliness that won her over. She wasn't sure whether she believed their ideas or not. After several visits they told her that there was an important week-long lecture series she must attend at Cleeve House in Wiltshire. It was some distance away, and when she argued that she couldn't go until she was done her studies, they insisted, saying it was the most important thing she could be doing. Finally she relented, and went away for a week. At that impressive house, she'd been so overwhelmed by the intensity of the sense of mission of all the brothers and sisters that she'd nearly agreed to quit her studies. Fortunately, she hadn't done that. Yet right after graduating, she'd begun living with the Family members, much to the anger and confusion of her parents. Did all this happen only four years ago? It seemed so much longer.

Father's voice pushes aside Sally's memories as he proclaims the third vow: "Do you pledge to inherit heavenly tradition, and as external persons of goodness, raise up your children as examples of this standard before your family and the universe?"

Again Kurt pumps his right hand, formed into a determined fist, emphatically as he joins with the others in shouting "Yes!" to Father's question. Sally echoes them faintly.

At the Holy Wine Ceremony, an elderly Korean man had passed them a tray containing small glasses of Holy Wine. She'd bowed to him in the Oriental manner, then taken one of the small glasses, from which she drank half of the wine, and then passed the remainder to Kurt, who'd bowed to her before finishing the wine. He then gave the glass back to her, and she'd bowed before giving the cup back to the Korean elder. In that moment, her Original Sin had been conditionally removed (provided she remained loyal to Father throughout her life), and any children born of their marriage would be sinless. But as they left the ballroom afterwards, Kurt had whispered something surprising and unsettling to her.

"I think there was perfume in the Holy Wine. Anyway, I'd rather drink beer." And he'd chuckled.

Sally had never touched a drop of alcohol since joining the church, believing it was forbidden, so she was confused by his remark and asked him to explain, but he shrugged it off. Later, when they went by subway to Queens to see the place where he worked, she noticed he'd hidden a case of beer in the closet where he kept his overalls and work clothes. When she asked him about it, he abruptly closed the closet door and told her that sometimes his co-workers made him nervous so he needed beer to relax. Do you do this often, she'd asked. He admitted he did it nearly every day. "There's this hallway upstairs in the back where nobody ever goes. I go up there and set up six of them in a row, then just toss them down, all at once. That's how you get the best hit."

"Don't your central figures know?"

"They don't hang around here much. I never do it if they're around."

Did God choose her to be Kurt's wife so she could save him from his drinking? Father had said that Blessed spouses were supposed to be Messiahs to each other, but Sally doubted she was up to this task.

Sally hears Father proclaiming the fourth and final vow now, his voice booming out over the arena. "Do you pledge to be centers of love before your societies, nations, the world and the universe, based upon the ideal family?"

"Yes!" all 2,075 couples roar, as one. Again Kurt punches the air with his right fist as he roars his assent, and again Sally joins in, though she feels her throat constricting, as though it wanted to cut off the word.

All the couples turn to face each other for the exchange of rings. Kurt reaches into his breast pocket and pulls out two gold bands, each embossed with a symbol representing the Twelve Gates of Heaven. Sally extends her right hand to Kurt and he slides one of the gold bands over her middle finger. Kurt then hands Sally the other ring, and she grasps his right hand in her left and slides the gold band onto his middle finger. The ceremony is almost complete.

Father closes the ceremony the way most church events end: with three cheers of "Mansei!" Looking elated, the rotund, white-robed Messiah crouches slightly and places his hands just above his knees, like a football coach about to lead his team in a cheer. All the brides and grooms follow his example. And then his voice booms out, "Aboji!" (meaning "Father!") The next instant all the newlyweds rise to their full height and fling their hands above their heads, shouting, "Mansei!" (meaning "Victory for Ten Thousand Years!").

Again Father squats while all the brides and grooms do likewise, placing their hands just above their knees. Again he gave the signal: "Aboji!" and again, the arena is filled with arms flinging heavenward as their response rings through the rafters: "Mansei!" And then a third time -- first the crouch, then the signal -- "Aboji!" followed by the uproarious cry: "Mansei!"

The True Parents are standing together now at the front of the dais in their robes of white and gold, being presented with elaborate floral bouquets as a symbol of thanks. They are the only hope to save mankind. Their marriage in 1960 was the fulfillment of the prophecy in *Revelation* about the Marriage of the Lamb. On that holy occasion, Father surpassed the accomplishments of Jesus Christ, who had been killed before he was able to marry. The crucifixion had foiled God's plans and postponed the arrival of the Kingdom of Heaven on Earth for 2,000 years. Now, Father could complete Jesus' work.

But these thoughts were no comfort to Sally. For a moment, she had an impulse to push all the other couples aside and run out of the arena, away from Kurt. But she knew this was a temptation from an evil spirit trying to stop her from receiving God's ultimate Blessing. In any case, there would be a wait of at least three years before she was to start her family with Kurt. During those three years, they must live apart -- Kurt in America and Sally in England -- and they must each recruit three new members into the Unification Church. Would Kurt change during those three years, as a result of the Holy Wine Ceremony? Would he become the kind of man that Sally would want to marry? Sally realizes that in any case she has no choice: Father has chosen Kurt for her and expects her to live up to her vows. Perhaps God wanted her to endure this difficult marriage so she could pay indemnity for the sins of all mankind.

Just then the band strikes up the wedding march and the couples begin filing out of the arena, two by two, with each bride slipping her hand into the crook of each groom's arm. The band switches to a church hymn, "The Song of the Banquet," which was written specifically about the Blessing ceremony. When it is their turn to leave, Sally and Kurt move to the exit. An older couple, who had been Blessed in an earlier ceremony, stand near the exit, loudly sighing in appreciation, as though admiring the exquisiteness of Father's matchmaking abilities. They gasp with pleasure when Sally and Kurt pass by.

Suddenly they exit onto Eighth Avenue, where they are bathed in the glare of the mid-day sun and blasted by hot July air. Startled pedestrians stop to watch the surreal spectacle of hundreds of brides and grooms strolling towards the corner of 33rd Street. A few bystanders ask to see the Blessing ring, and Kurt and Sally hold out their hands for them to see.

"Very nice!" they tell her.

"Whew, I'm glad that's over with," Kurt says over his shoulder to her when they reach the next corner. "Let's get something to eat."

He jerks his head in the direction of the McDonald's restaurant across the street from the World Mission Center. Sally follows him through the door, carefully removing her wedding veil and carrying it in one hand. For an instant, she pictures herself trailing behind Kurt all her life, still wearing her hand-made wedding dress, following him into dingy bars and greasy mechanic shops. Normally, she would never consent to eat at a fast food place. But wasn't this, after all, the way things would have to be from now on?

The Work

"*SERVIAM*," I WHISPER, as my lips meet the floor. "I will serve." I can hear the footsteps of the director fading down the corridor as I rise to my feet again. Ten seconds ago she called out, "Rose! Wake up!" as she rapped on my door. Now I hear her knocking on a different door, calling the name of another girl, and then continuing down the hall. It is 5:40 a.m.

The sun is beaming through the window into my room. It's a bright, cheerful April morning – just what I need to lift my spirits. Mid-term exams at Boston College are coming up and I'm worried because I've had so little time to study. Even so, this fine weather comforts me somehow.

Warm spring days always remind me of my Auntie Flo – my mother's sister who was a nun – and how she used to visit us when I was a little girl. Auntie Flo was the only one in my family who ever seemed to have time for me. The rest of my family favored my brother Stephen. I think she was hoping I'd become a nun just like her, but my mom and dad were dead set against that idea. She would come on the bus to our house in Somerville and then take me to the South End, where we always stopped at the Cathedral of the Holy Cross. We'd get there just in time to pray the noon hour Angelus. Auntie Flo would say the words aloud and I'd join in for the Hail Mary. All the time we were praying I looked up at all these great stained glass windows with the pictures of the saints and the Holy Family, and I got this really peaceful feeling inside.

After we were finished praying Auntie Flo used to take me on the bus to Boston Common. We'd always stop first at one of the Brigham's restaurants close to the Common so she could buy ice cream. Then we'd walk through the Public Garden licking our ice cream cones. Auntie Flo would take her last little bit of cone and toss it into the pond for the fish to eat, and I always did the same.

I realize that I'm dawdling by the window thinking about Auntie Flo. I turn away from the window and open the drawer to the nightstand beside my bed, reaching in to grasp the "discipline" – a small whip made from white knotted cord. I take it with me to the shower, turn the water to the coldest setting and let it run for a moment before I step into the icy stream. I try to imagine all the sin bound up within my flesh becoming frozen into icicles and flaking away from my skin. While I soap myself I pray for the success of the head prelate and that the Holy Father in Rome will allow him all the latitude he needs to accomplish The Work of God – *Opus Dei*. Before I turn off the water I pick up the discipline and begin my prayer: "Hail Mary, full of grace, the Lord is with you," I whisper, flailing the discipline back over my shoulders to lash my buttocks. "Blessed are you among women and blessed is the fruit of your womb," I continue, whipping myself again and again. "Holy Mary, mother of God, pray for us sinners, now and at the hour of our death." I continue striking until the prayer is finished.

"They're for the mortification of the flesh." That's what the director told me ten months ago as she handed me the discipline and its even crueler sister, the cilice. I was shocked when she gave them to me, but I've grown used to these two necessities which keep my stubborn body from falling prey to its basest instincts and lusts. After toweling myself dry I replace the discipline in the drawer. It will not be needed again for another week.

It's time now to dress for meditation with all the other female numeraries – full-time members of Opus Dei – which will be followed by the Latin Mass. I dress mechanically, my mind already racing ahead to my day at school. I'm looking forward to my first class: English Poetry. The professor has been lecturing for several weeks on the Romantics; today he will begin discussing the Victorian poets.

Originally I'd intended to take a class in modern French literature, but when I told the director what I was going to study she asked to see the syllabus. When I brought it to her, she turned pale. "Flaubert," she read aloud. "Balzac. Victor Hugo, *Les Misérables*. But Rose, these are all banned works!" So I chose something safer, and settled on English Poetry instead.

Now I'm glad I decided on the poetry course, because Beth will be there. I always look forward to seeing her. She reminds me of the way I used to be a year ago – a smart first year student jumping ahead to the advanced courses. In fact that's how I met Nancy, the numerary who inspired me to join Opus Dei. She was a sophomore and became my best friend during my freshman year. We used to go to the cafeteria after class and discuss all kinds of things. Nancy convinced me to attend some Opus Dei events and she kept encouraging me to take my faith more seriously. My parents are half-hearted Catholics, so before I met Nancy the most I ever did was go to mass most Sundays.

Nancy told me that God needed me to give a much greater commitment to The Work. We used to pray together. But as soon as I "whistled" – that's what we call it when somebody joins – Nancy stopped meeting me after class and I saw her talking to someone else. Now I hardly see her anymore. But I suppose that's just how it has to be, if we're going to gather as many people as possible to do God's Work.

After mass, I return to my room and carefully wrap the cilice around my upper thigh before I head down to breakfast. The cilice is a wide band resembling a loose chain with sharp points protruding from every link. I strap it on so that all the points dig into my flesh. They break the skin only slightly, unless I bump it, but I never go to public swimming pools any more. I don't want people to see the tiny gashes it leaves. The time is now a quarter to eight and for the next two hours the cilice will be my protector, admonishing my body to stay obedient to God. I'll only take it off when I leave for class.

We are allotted only fifteen minutes for breakfast, and then we must begin our assigned cleaning tasks. Today my chore is to vacuum and dust two rooms while wearing my white uniform – the prestigious uniform of a full-time celibate member of Opus Dei. It is a reminder to everyone of my greater commitment to The Work. Some of the female numeraries have been assigned to clean the rooms of the male numeraries, but they must never speak to them while they are doing these chores, nor must the men ever speak to them – not even to say, "Thanks." Fortunately my assignment is to clean some rooms on my own floor so I won't have to face that temptation.

When my chores are done, I change and go to meet the director for our weekly chat. During these meetings we discuss any doubts I may be having, whether I've been praying and saying rosary as often as I'm supposed to, and we confer about the girls I'm trying to draw closer to Opus Dei. The director reminds me of how essential it is for me to do exactly what God wants and to go exactly where God needs me to go if I hope to receive His complete blessing. Today I tell the director everything I know about Beth, and how I'm planning to ask her to come with me tomorrow to my volunteer project with inner city students in Roxbury. I'm tutoring young African-American girls in writing skills, and I'm hoping Beth will come along so I can witness to her about Opus Dei. Beth is a good, idealistic girl who admires my volunteer work and will probably be glad to come along. The director approves my plan.

At the end of the meeting I run upstairs to take off the cilice and grab my books. Luckily, there's an empty seat on the Commonwealth Avenue bus, so I'm able to read on my way to class. Only religious books from pre-Vatican II authors are supposed to be read during this journey; if I need to study for school, I must do it later. I've chosen a book by the founder of Opus Dei, Father Escriva.

I'm just barely in time for the class. Most of the lecture hall has already filled up, but I spot Beth right away sitting down near the front. As always, I admire her smartly bobbed black hair and fashionable eyeglasses that make her look perky and intelligent. When she sees me come through the door she waves and points to the seat she saved right beside her.

"Hey, Rose! I was beginning to worry you weren't going to make it!"

"Hey, Beth! Thanks!" I sit down beside her and rummage around in my backpack for the poetry anthology. Beth spots the book I've been carrying and picks it up. "Escriva," she says, her brows furrowing. "Isn't that the guy who started your spiritual group?"

"Father Escriva, that's right. He's the founder of Opus Dei." I quickly tuck the book away in my bag. It's better if Beth doesn't find out too much too quickly, or it might scare her off. I'm reminded of the song, "La Pesca Submarina," which we often sing at our meetings. We sing it in Spanish but the English translation goes something like this:

As for me, I like to fish, but I like underwater fishing best!
To go after those fish is a divine thing!
As for me, I like to fish without a hook, and without a fish line;
This waiting for the fish to bite, it's not for me, no, it's not for me!

I picture myself swimming to the depths of the ocean in my quest to capture Beth. God has called her to a vocation in Opus Dei, but she doesn't know it yet so I must try to snare her before someone from another faith can hook her and cause her to be lost forever to Our Father in heaven.

The lecture today is about Gerard Manley Hopkins, one of my favourite poets. I thrill as I listen to the glorious words from "God's Grandeur," despite the professor's dry, pedantic manner of reading:

"And for all this, nature is never spent;
There lives the dearest freshness deep down things;
And though the last lights off the black West went,
Oh, morning, at the brown brink eastward, springs –
Because the Holy Ghost over the bent
World broods with warm breast, and with, ah! bright wings."

After the class Beth and I have a couple of hours before our next classes so we leave together and go to pray the Angelus and to have lunch. It's such a beautiful day that we decide to get our sandwiches at the cafeteria and take them with us to Chestnut Hill Park. It's right next to the campus, several acres of park surrounding a large reservoir. Many of the students like to go there to sit on the grass while they study or eat lunch.

Beth comes from a good Catholic background, but, just like me one year ago, she doesn't take it too seriously. When I first suggested that we meet at noon to pray the Angelus, she looked like she was trying to hold back a laugh. She told me she hadn't done that since grade school. But I knew that in her heart Beth was a good and devout girl, so I convinced her that saying these traditional prayers is a good way to purify the heart.

I begin: "The angel of the Lord appeared unto Mary."

Beth responds: "And she conceived of the Holy Spirit."

And then together we say, "Hail Mary, full of grace ..." and continue to the end of the prayer. As soon as the final "Amen" is spoken, Beth flops back on the grass, not caring about whether she might stain her shirt and jeans.

"Whew!" she sighs. "Are you ready for your mid-terms?" Leaning back on her elbows, she raises her face toward the warm sun and closes her eyes to savor it. "I'm not, I'm gonna have to study like mad this weekend!" She doesn't seem worried though; she's a good student, I bet she'll ace all her exams. How I'll do is another matter. But I'd better not worry about that or it might stir up doubts which I'd then have to report to the director and confess to the priest.

"By the way," Beth goes on, still lolling her head back to enjoy the sun, "did you see that guy in class this morning that kept looking back at us from the front row? He was checking you out, Rose! You should talk to him some time."

"I bet he was checking *you* out, you're the cute one," I told her quickly, hoping to change the subject.

"Oh, come on, Rose! Have you looked in a mirror lately? Long brown hair with big brown eyes to match! Lots of guys really like that sweet innocent look you have with your granny dresses and no makeup." Beth turns over on her stomach and gazes straight at me now. "Nope, I'm sure he was giving you the eye. I saw him! Three times! The last time I caught him looking I gave him a wink and jerked my head in your direction. But of course you were off in your own world somewhere. You didn't see a thing." Beth let out one of her long uninhibited laughs.

I couldn't help asking, "So what did he do? Did he wink back?"

"Nah, he just got all embarrassed and turned away and didn't look back again for the rest of the class." And she gave her hearty laugh again. That's one of the things I really like about Beth; her ready humor and spontaneity.

I toss the crust from my sandwich into the reservoir. An orange and black carp rises slowly to the surface and nibbles at it lazily. Beth follows my example and tosses a scrap from her own sandwich toward the reservoir, but a seagull swoops down and nabs it before it touches the water.

Beth turns over onto her stomach so she can look at me again. "So Rose, what do you do about dating in that group of yours? Are you only allowed to date each other or something?"

I don't want to tell Beth about the celibacy vow I made when I became a numerary, because she isn't ready to understand that yet. I change the subject.

"You know, Beth, I'm going out to Roxbury tomorrow to teach literacy skills in this volunteer project and I was wondering ..."

But she persists. "No, I really want to know, Rose. What do you do if a guy wants to go out with you or you with him? Could you talk to that guy in English Poetry or are you supposed to just ignore him or whatever? I mean, even if he's a Catholic, does he have to join Opus Dei before you can date him?"

I'll have to find a way to dodge around the question. "I'm focusing on my own spiritual growth right now, Beth, so I'm not dating anyone."

Beth rolls over on her back and looks up at the spring sky marked by just a few wisps of cloud. "You know, I admire, you, Rose. You're volunteering and you're helping people and you're trying so hard to live the right way. But what if you meet a really nice guy? What if he's not Opus Dei, maybe he's not even a Catholic? What do you do then?"

"I believe my vocation to Opus Dei is more important than anything. So I'd have to discourage him, I'm not allowed to go out with him."

"Not 'allowed'? You mean Opus Dei doesn't let you go out with *anyone*?"

I can't hide it any longer; I've got to tell her. "Yes, that's right, Beth. I've offered up all these desires to God so I can do The Work without distraction. So that means I'm not going to date anyone. Ever."

Beth lets out a low whistle. "Not *ever?* Then why don't you become a nun, if that's the way you feel? I thought that's what they did."

"Being a numerary for Opus Dei is better than being a nun. There's no waiting, no long period of contemplation, you just start right in doing God's work. I know I'm doing the right thing. I'm the happiest I've ever been."

I've said these words many times before to my parents, when they questioned me about my decision to join Opus Dei. But somehow this time they don't sound convincing – not even to me. I wish I could feel perfectly at peace, the way I used to when I was a little girl walking with Auntie Flo. Instead I just feel how hard I've got to work to keep up with everything God expects of me.

Beth is studying me now. "Look, Rose, I really like you. You talk about things most girls never talk about and you're really trying to make the world a better place. I admire that in you. But I just don't think you're happy. That's not what I see. In fact, to be perfectly honest, you look like you're having a hard time."

I feel tears starting at the backs of my eyes, so I put up my hand as if I'm shielding them from the sun. Somehow, Beth has found out my deepest feelings. I hadn't even dared to admit it to myself until she said it. But it's true, I *am* having a hard time. Suddenly I feel such love for Beth. I know she's a good-hearted girl, God must surely have called her to The Work. But when I try to picture Beth as a numerary for Opus Dei, I don't like the image I get. She'd have to change her haircut and her eyeglasses. I imagine her going to confession, and then cleaning house while wearing the cilice. Somehow I knew that if she was to do all that, she just wouldn't be the same anymore. Not the same Beth who just a moment ago saw so clearly into my heart. And then I understand that I just can't do that to her. I can't stand the thought.

"No, I'm fine, Beth. Really I am. Everything's great, really." I'm overcome by a desire to get away from Beth so I can think about what she just said. "Look how late it is!" I exclaim, jumping to my feet. "We've got a class in half an hour!" I've decided not to bother inviting Beth to the volunteer project.

"Half an hour. Lots of time!" Beth comments, but she stands up with me, and we pick up our knapsacks and start heading back to the campus. "Oh man, what a gorgeous day!" she exults, spreading out her arms to embrace the scene. "Who cares about mid-terms when the weather's like this!"

We walk back to Boston College in silence. While we walk, I remember what Auntie Flo used to say to me whenever we left the park at the end of a fine spring day. While waiting for the bus to take us back home, she'd ask me: "Did you have fun, dear?" I always said, "Oh, yes, Auntie Flo! I love it when we go to the park. You're my most favorite person, *ever*." And then she'd put a finger to my lips and tell me in a way that was both kind and stern: "Hush, Rose, it's not me, it's God's love you're feeling. No matter what you do or where you go, God will always love you." And then I'd fall asleep with my head in her lap while we rode the bus back to Somerville.

Let's Get Lost

THE ROAD PAST MERCIFUL is only busy during tourist season, when cars go by on their way to the resorts and lakes. I'm not supposed to go near the highway, but I keep going there anyway. Usually I like to walk by the road because it's a good place to look for animals and birds, but today I've come here because I've got an idea I can't get out of my head.

The idea is this: if I really want to leave Merciful, all I have to do is walk down to the shoulder of that road and stick out my thumb. Right now I'm walking parallel to the road but a little away from it. I'm nervous about getting any closer to the road. I use two hands to lift the hem of my dress slightly, so it won't trail in the dirt when I step down into one of the hollows or gopher holes in the rough grass.

The turnoff onto the gravel road to Merciful is marked by big signs saying, PRIVATE PROPERTY. DO NOT ENTER. I have to walk past these signs to get here and then I can walk out onto the small hills at the base of the mountain. In the early summer, like right now, the grass gets dry and starts turning brown. I'm going to get dust all over my black patent leather shoes.

If I ran away from Merciful, that would be the worst sin I could commit. The Prophet says we should have as little as possible to do with the Gentiles. If a Gentile tries to talk to me while I'm out walking, I'm supposed to turn around without a word and run away, showing him only the back of my long white dress.

But today I don't have a choice. No matter what the Prophet says, I need the Gentiles' help. I've just turned fourteen, and that means I'm old enough to become a celestial wife. The Prophet left yesterday to go back to Utah, and he almost certainly left instructions with the file leader, Shem Filmore, about what should

73

be done with girls like me. If so, today I will be told the name of the man I'm to marry.

But now that I'm down near the road, I'm afraid to take that final step. The wind ruffles my hair and I can smell the delicate, earthy scent of the grasses as the last of the dew dries off them. I look down toward the road, but can't bring myself to go any closer, let alone start hitch-hiking. What if someone really terrible picks me up and something awful happens? Again and again Elder Filmore has warned us about the evils of the Gentiles. But I don't really want to go back to Merciful, either.

I don't want to be a celestial wife. At least, not yet.

Above me a hawk circles in the pale blue sky, watching out for hares, gophers, or mice. I squint from the sun, and can only make out the black and white markings on the hawk's brown wings as he circles the sky, keeping watch.

When I was a little girl I looked forward to becoming a celestial wife. I thought it would be a wonderful thing to become the wife of a godly man. When I was six or seven, I asked God to let me become the celestial wife of Shem Filmore. How wonderful it would be to marry the file leader, I thought. But that was before I got older—before I started walking by the highway.

The hawk must see something, because he is circling lower. Beyond me, I notice two hares leaping down the slope towards the coolness of the ditch beside the road. They see me and stop, but they haven't seen the hawk. I stop too, so I won't scare them, and stand perfectly still so they'll feel it's safe to keep going down to the ditch. After a moment they start moving again. I feel a momentary coolness even before I see the hawk's shadow sweeping over the grass.

If I've really got to marry someone, I'd marry Elder Filmore's son, Hugh. He's eighteen now and hasn't been given a wife yet. I've seen him looking at me like he likes me. He's sort of big and gangly and he has this wild red hair that sticks out from his head no matter how he combs it, but he's nice. Even so, what I really want to do is stay in school and not have to marry anyone until later.

The hares sense that the hawk is closing in on them now. One of them's staying still, while the other's darting towards the highway. I'm afraid it might run out in front of a car, but after it climbs up from the ditch onto the shoulder, it stops. A couple of cars rush by, and it doesn't move. The hawk ignores it, and circles above the one left behind, which is now springing back up the slope.

If I can just get to Cresthaven, I can look for Auntie Ruth. She used to be one of us, but now she lives with the Gentiles. People say awful things about her, but I remember her when she was at Merciful. Before she left she was one of Elder Filmore's celestial wives. I bet she'd help me stay in school. But would she take me in if I just showed up on her doorstep? I think I should write to her first. I wish I could telephone her but the only phone is at Daddy's main house where everyone would be listening.

The hare by the road turns back and is going up the slope behind the other one. But it's too late. The hawk plunges so suddenly, I don't see it until it strikes. The hare screams as the talons enter her sides. I let out a yelp of my own. The other hare bounds off up the slope and away.

For a moment the hawk and the dying hare are a frenzy of wings and fur and slashing beaks and claws. Then the hare lies still. I turn away and look back toward the road.

Soon I see a car filled with Gentiles coming, a young family with two children in the back seat, enough room for me. I'm still too afraid to stick out my thumb. Instead I turn away and when the kids wave to me, I don't wave back. I make up my mind to try to contact Auntie Ruth before I run away from Merciful. I have to let her know what I'm planning.

While I'm walking along the gravel road, I go right past the two big signs, and later, I pass another sign made of white stones set in the dirt. This sign says, "KEEP SWEET," which means stay quiet, don't complain, be happy. But I don't think I can keep sweet anymore. Not since I noticed Hugh looking at me. That's when I started thinking I'd like to decide for myself who I'll marry.

The gravel road passes by the school and houses and ends in front of the main meeting hall. I'm walking past one of the houses of Elder Filmore and I see Florence and Bathsheba and some of their kids in the backyard. Flo and Beth are hanging up the wash on the clotheslines. It's a fine day for hanging clothes out, with only a little wind and lots of heat. I wave and Flo waves back. She's expecting another baby soon and so she moves awkwardly, her stomach bulging. That baby will be Elder Filmore's nineteenth child.

It used to be the rule that girls didn't get married until they were sixteen, but lately they're marrying girls younger than that. The elders like my looks—I've seen them looking—I'm tall for my age, and slender, with long blonde hair that I keep tied up at the back. I've got high cheek bones and delicate features. Some say I'm the prettiest of all the girls of marrying age. I wish I weren't. Then maybe they'd let me stay in school.

I go to the house where Rebekah, Leah and their children live. It's a plain white two-story house. There are other houses like it nearby clustered around a grassy area with a sandbox and a slide and some swings in the middle. When I get close to the house, Diana—that's my sister, she's twelve—runs right past me and we nearly bump into each other. At the sight of her I start worrying the Prophet might have left instructions about her, too. But no, he wouldn't do that, would he? She's way too young to be a celestial wife. Or is she?

"Hi, Tamar!" she yells, giving me a wave. She almost trips over a toy car one of the little boys left on the sidewalk. I grab her before she can fall and pull her up straight.

"Look where you're going!" I scold, but I don't really feel mad because she's laughing her head off. Zach Filmore is chasing her for a joke and she's taking him on a wild goose chase all over Merciful.

I let her go and she takes off again, yelling, "Bye, Tamar!" and heads for the road, with Zach laughing and following close behind.

I pick up the toy car, half-squished from Diana's foot, and take it with me inside the house, because Daddy always gets angry if he sees toys lying around. "Mother, I'm back!" I shout into the house, but instead of hearing the voice of my mother Rebekah answering, I hear my celestial mother Leah calling from out back. "Oh, there you are, Tamar. Where did you get to?"

I walk through the house to the back door and find Leah sitting in a lawn chair holding her baby, Hannah, in her lap. She has long black hair tied up at the back and is wearing a blue gingham dress with puffed-out shoulders. Hannah is sucking on a bottle with her eyes closed, staying quiet. I sit down next to her in a lawn chair and look out at the playground where a lot of the young kids are running around shouting at each other.

"I was out for a walk."

"Not down by the highway again, I hope."

"I was just walking." I start to get up again.

"Sit down, Tamar," she says sharply. I do. "The Prophet has chosen the man you're going to marry. You need to prepare yourself."

I scowl down at my feet in their dusty black leather shoes, sticking out in front of me on the lawn chair. "You're not my real mother," I tell her. "Where's Sister Rebekah? She's the one who should tell me this."

"Rebekah's gone to town with Hugh Filmore to pick up groceries for the families." When she says the "families" she means all of my father's five families. "Anyway, I'm also your mother in the eyes of God. There's no call to be rude, Tamar."

"I'm sorry. So who did the Prophet decide will be my husband?" My father should be the one to tell me this, but he's away in the field and I know Leah's dying to tell me.

"Elder Shem Filmore. Tamar, you're going to be the celestial wife of the file leader! You'll have a wonderful place in heaven."

Leah is looking at me sideways. She's trying to guess what I'm thinking. I'll bet she has a pretty good idea. She says softly, "Don't worry, Tamar. Before I was married, I was scared, too. When I was chosen to marry your father, I was a young girl not much older than you. But look how well everything's worked out."

I hear the sound of a van pulling up in front of the house. It must be Hugh bringing my mother Rebekah back from Cresthaven with the groceries. Then I hear the sound of the van's back doors opening and bags being unloaded. I run inside to help. Mother calls out to me from inside the van while she's handing out the sacks: "Well, look who's here! Miss Nature Lover's paying us a visit! I could've used a hand at the grocery store, you know. Did you see anything interesting today?" She's pretending to be mad but I can tell she isn't really. Mother loves animals and birds too. She likes to hear me talk about them.

"I saw a hawk today, and two hares," I say, but then I stop. I don't want to tell her that story. I quickly turn, carrying two sacks and almost bump into Hugh, who's standing behind me holding open the van's back doors.

"What's the rush, Tammy?"

"Nothing, Hugh." I duck under his arms and hurry towards the door.

"Here, let me take those bags." He holds out his big hands to me.

"No, I'm fine. Get your own bags!" I dodge out of his reach.

Hugh chuckles and follows me into the house with two more bags. Mother's voice comes from the back yard, saying something to Leah. She must've decided to leave it up to Hugh to unpack the groceries. Mother's jealous of Leah because Daddy favors her, but she covers it up by trying to be extra nice to her. I can't make out what they're saying.

Hugh walks past me into the kitchen and starts unpacking the groceries and putting them away. "I can take care of that, Hugh," I tell him. "You've got more important things to do."

He shrugs and keeps putting them away. "Not right now. They've given me the van for the afternoon. How'd you like to go to town for ice cream?"

I stare at him, amazed. He must have heard the news. It would be improper at any time for him to take me into town unless we were going with a group of people. But now that the Prophet has decided I'm supposed to marry his father, it's out of the question.

"You know the Prophet has chosen me to marry your father, right?"

"Yeah, I know." He makes a face. "Congratulations."

"Hugh! Aren't you scared of getting in trouble?"

He walks over to me so he can speak very softly without being overheard.

"Listen, Tammy. Your mother and Leah are busy out back. If we drive into town right now, you can do whatever you have to do."

So he's guessed that I want to get away. And if he knows, who else knows? But if Hugh takes me into Cresthaven, I can call Auntie Ruth.

"Okay, let me finish this up and then I'll go."

Hugh waves as if to say, drop that. "Let's get while the getting's good."

He gets behind the wheel and backs the old panel van down the driveway and soon we pass the KEEP SWEET sign, and then the bigger ones to keep away the Gentiles. We're in town in fifteen minutes. It's not a long drive.

Hugh cruises down the full length of the main drag. It takes maybe five minutes to do this, and then he asks, "You want to go for ice cream right away or maybe just drive around a bit?" I know he wants to keep driving so I tell him to go right ahead and he goes back out onto the highway again. We get going a really good speed, just like the tourists, as if we were heading on to Castlegar. The sun is baking the countryside. It's dry and stark, like everything is standing out in sharp relief. I crank down the window and rest my right arm on the door, letting the sun warm my skin through the cloth. The mountains are going by and I'm trying to spot coyotes or deer out the window, but all I can make out is the skittering of ground squirrels through the dry grass. Far away to the west I can see a couple of eagles up in the sky, watching over everything.

"You know what I'm thinking?" Hugh looks over at me for a moment, then back at the road.

"What?" I try to guess.

"I'm thinking we should just forget about Merciful and keep on driving."

"Where would we go?"

"Vancouver."

"Vancouver? What for?"

"Just to get away. I've got some money to carry us for a while."

"But what would we do?"

"Look. You don't want to marry Dad, right?"

I don't answer.

"You don't have to say. Anyway, listen, Tammy. I made a big mistake last week. Big, big mistake." He slaps the dashboard with his right hand.

"Mistake? What did you do?"

"I told Dad that now that I'm old enough, I want to marry you."

I clasp my hands in my lap and look down at them. I don't want to marry either of them. I want to go to school. Finally I ask, "So what did he say?"

Hugh waves his hand, but doesn't say anything for a moment. We're going faster than the speed limit and I wonder if I should mention it.

"He told me I was speaking out of my proper place and that he's going to tell the Prophet to send me on a mission to straighten out my attitude."

"A mission? Like to Utah or Arizona or something?"

"Something like that. But here's what I think. He's just getting rid of me so he can have you. The same thing happened to Simon Cartwright, remember? When he was old enough to get married, they sent him away, too."

"He was the one that wanted to marry Esther, right?"

"Right. But Elder Thornton wanted Esther."

Hugh notices how fast he's driving and slows down a little. I think about what would happen if I told Hugh, "Okay, let's do it." It probably wouldn't even work. How far would we get before they figured out we were gone and called the police? Could we stay lost for long, with me underage? How would we explain it?

On the other hand, what did I have to lose? If I called Auntie Ruth, she might not be able to take me in, since she lives so close to Merciful. The elders might give her a lot of trouble. And how could I repay her, if I just showed up like that? That plan might not work either.

"I've got to warn you about something, though," Hugh says after a while.

I look up and wait.

"If you run away, they might just replace you with somebody else. Somebody younger."

"Younger?"

"Yeah. Like Diana."

"Diana!" I gasp. "Oh, my God, Hugh. They wouldn't do that, would they?"

Hugh shrugs. "I've heard father saying that the Prophet wants to start marrying off girls before they can get rebellious."

Diana. One time when she was little, she was crying because she was scared of a thunderstorm, and I hugged her and promised her I would protect her forever. Suddenly, I feel desperate for her.

"Hugh, could we sneak back and grab Diana, and take her with us?"

"Tammy, there's no time! If we're going to do this, we've got to go now."

I sit for a moment. For some reason, I keep thinking about what I saw this morning, when the hawk caught the hare. I picture Leah telling Diana that she is going to be sealed to the file leader. But if I rush back to protect Diana, wouldn't something like that happen to her anyway eventually? In a few years' time, we'd both be sitting in lawn chairs beside Leah. Both of us pregnant.

Hugh keeps driving west, while glancing over at me occasionally. At last I wave my hand in the direction of the road ahead.

"All right, Hugh. Let's go. Let's get lost."

Merciful Flight

HUGH BARELY SLOWS DOWN as we swing through the curve. The stone walls of the Kootenay Pass rise up on both sides of the road. It's been less than an hour. We've hardly said a word.

"How long do you think it'll take before the elders see we're gone?"

Hugh looks at me and shrugs. "I think they'll be too surprised to figure it out right away. By the time they do, we'll be long gone."

"But I'm supposed to be sealed to your father tomorrow. They'll be looking for me."

Hugh doesn't answer. It's mid-afternoon in late summer. The sun's still high in the sky. We pass a sign giving the distance to Salmo, Castlegar ... and Vancouver.

Vancouver. The place where we're going to get lost.

Finally, Hugh says, "Tamar, I have something to tell you. While I was helping your mother get groceries in Cresthaven, I sneaked away and called Auntie Ruth."

"Auntie Ruth!" She's the only person I know who could help us. She used to be one of the ten wives of the file leader. Now she helps girls like me who need to get away from Merciful.

"Mother didn't know?"

"She thought I was in the bathroom. Ruth gave me a phone number to call in Vancouver. She said these people can give us a place to stay, or get us a lawyer or whatever, if we need it. In case the elders try to make us go back." He reaches into his breast pocket and sets down a slip of paper on the dashboard. It's written in pencil on a scrap of brown paper from a grocery bag. I pick it up and memorize the number, then give it back to Hugh.

"We're going to need it."

❧❦❧

At Christina Lake Provincial Park, the road travels along the lake shore for part of the way south, almost to the U.S. border. It's a beautiful, narrow strip of blue with forest all around. The sun is getting lower now and when we turn back west at the town of Christina Lake, Hugh lowers the visor to keep it from shining in his eyes.

"Here, Tammy, do something useful. Find out if they're talking about us," he snaps, stabbing his finger at the radio. I think he's annoyed because I've just been sitting back, looking around. I've never been this far from Merciful before.

I turn the radio on and start twisting the dial. There's nothing from close by but after a while I pick up a rock station out of Penticton.

"Not that," Hugh says, lifting one hand from the wheel to make a dismissive wave. "Try to get Trail or something. See if they're telling people to watch out for us."

But I don't find anything, and after a while I give up and turn the radio off again.

❧❧❧

I'm sleeping with my head against the window when I feel the van slowing down and pulling over onto a side road. I wake up, confused about where I am for a moment, then I see Hugh looking at me, smiling, and I remember.

"I'm sorry I got mad at you earlier, honeybun." He's never called me anything like that before. "It's just all this worry, you know. Anyway, how about we get something to eat?" We're outside a truck stop diner in Osoyoos.

We sit at the counter on red vinyl-covered stools and a big, older woman with heavy make-up comes over to serve us. We both ask for lemonade. The name tag on her shirt says, "Bernie." She sets the menus in front of us and comes back with our drinks.

"Here you go, sweetheart," she says, putting a glass down in front of me. She gives Hugh a long look when she sets his glass down.

He looks away, embarrassed.

"If anybody asks," he whispers after Bernie leaves, "just say you're my sister."

"It's our clothes," I whisper back. "They give us away. We should change or something."

Hugh shrugs. "Into what? Anyway, we haven't got time." He asks Bernie for a hamburger and fries, and we share it.

As we're leaving the truck stop, we see a fruit stand by the road, selling apples. Hugh stops, and we buy a bag.

❧❧❧

Near Keremeos the sun drops behind the mountains and it suddenly feels cooler and somehow stranger driving around with Hugh. We don't even have a clear idea what we'll do when we get to Vancouver. The whole thing's starting to look really crazy. I look over at Hugh.

"What's the matter?" He sees the way I'm looking.

"This'll never work. If they find us you'll be arrested. And no matter what I say, they won't believe me."

"They'll have to catch us first!" Hugh laughs, all bravado, but I can see the look behind his eyes before he turns his head and looks out the driver's side window. He's scared. He was in trouble with the elders before, but now he's in it up to his eyebrows. And there's nothing I can do.

"Hugh?" I say, trying to offer him something.

"What, sweetie?"

"Let's not stop again until we get to Vancouver. I mean, if we can help it. I didn't like the way that waitress looked at us back there."

❧❧❧

It's midnight and we're just coming into Princeton. For the last hour I've been struggling to stay awake for Hugh's sake, but when I feel the van slow down I realize I've been asleep for a while. Hugh pulls the van onto the shoulder and stops. Ahead of us I see a red neon "VACANCY" sign lit up in front of a small tourist motel. Beside the Vacancy sign, there is a tall sign shaped like a silver sword, turning back and forth in the wind. The words "Treasure

Island Hideaway" are written down the length of the blade. Hugh turns to me.

"Crouch down under the dashboard so no-one can see you. I'm going to register like I'm alone. Then I'll sneak you in."

"Hugh, shouldn't we just keep going?"

"I can't stay awake. I've got to rest or I can't drive."

I do what he says and we pull into the motel courtyard. Hugh goes in to register and then comes out a few minutes later with the key. He drives the van over to the cottage, very close to the door so no-one from the motel office can see who's going inside.

"Quick, slide in there," Hugh commands when the door's open. I crouch down and rush inside. Hugh makes like he's opening the back of the van to get out some luggage, though we haven't got any. Then he slams shut the door and parks the van properly. I sit on the bed and wait for him.

"Well, honey, here we are," he says with a half smile when he comes back in. He sets the bag of apples beside me on the nightstand. I wonder what he's planning to do. There's only one bed. He sees me looking at him with that question in my eyes.

"Don't worry," he tells me. "I won't touch you unless you want me to. I just need to sleep." He slumps down in a chair.

I look at him and I feel something stirring inside me. This is the first time I've been alone with a man other than my father. Hugh looks handsome, with his red hair flying away from his face in all directions, his big hands clasped together in his lap, his head leaning back against the wall. He looks so tired I wonder if he's going to fall asleep right there in the chair. And I think, why not let him lie down here beside me?

I pat the bedspread beside me and say softly, "Why don't you lie down here, Hugh? You look so tired."

Hugh beams broadly and flops down on the bed next to me. He lies back on the pillow and looks over at me like he's looking at something rare and wonderful.

"You sure are pretty, Tammy. You've got to be the prettiest girl in Merciful. Maybe you're the prettiest in the world."

I redden and laugh, then look away and stand up. I turn back to face him. "You going to fall asleep like that, or do you want to get undressed? I could go to the bathroom and wait until you've taken off your clothes and got under the covers."

"Okay." I wait until I hear him call to say he's ready.

Meanwhile I've taken off my dress and stockings and I'm just in my underwear. I creep back into the room and lie down next to him, on top of the covers.

"Don't worry," he says again. He takes my hand and holds it. "We're going to get away. They're not going to find us."

I pull my hand free and get under the covers. Then I roll over to face him, and I see that he's already rolled over to face me. Our heads are close together on the pillow and for a moment I think he's going to kiss me. But instead he just smiles. I sort of want him to kiss me, and yet I don't. But I like having him here, big and warm in the bed beside me. "Hugh," I whisper hesitantly after a minute. "If we ... you know, if we did it. That would mean your father couldn't marry me, right?"

After a long pause, he says, "Yeah, I guess." He doesn't move. "But do you want to, Tammy?" Then he reaches his hand out towards me, slowly.

I don't know what to think any more. I'm tired of thinking. I'm tired of everything. I just want to get away.

"Yes," I say, and I move towards him.

❧❧❧

My eyes open when the first light filters through the window blinds. The clock on the nightstand says six o'clock. Then I look back at Hugh, sleeping beside me, with one had still touching my arm. In the half-light of morning, he looks so beautiful and sad. He wakes up as if he knows I'm looking at him, and he gapes at me with both wonder and alarm.

"Tamar, we'd better get going. They're looking for us."

I sit up, still holding the sheets over me, and take an apple from the nightstand. "I guess this is breakfast," I say. I take a bite, then hand it to him. He eagerly finishes it.

"That was good." We both get out of bed, and for a moment we are surprised and ashamed to see each other naked. Quickly we cover ourselves with sheets again.

With a sudden flash of insight, I understand that I have turned a corner in my life, and nothing will ever be the same again.

We get ready, and leave as fast as we can. Hugh starts driving west again. I stick my head out the window to watch the little motel shrinking behind us. The "Treasure Island Hideaway" sign is turning every way in the wind, its silver edges glinting out a warning or a curse.

Fair Game

ONE TINY RED CIRCLE OF LIGHT – the glowing end of a cigarette in the window of a parked car – told Rick everything he needed to know. They were watching him again.

The rain fell steadily on his plain black umbrella as it had done whenever he'd been out that day. Another typical Vancouver winter day – no surprises there. The Victoria Drive trolley bus had been moist and steamy; all the windows were speckled with condensation, and rivulets of water trickled down the runnels on the rubber floor mat. Rick had dismounted at Vanness and turned down Stainsbury to walk to his basement suite. That's when he noticed them, parked across the street.

There must be two men in that car, Rick thought, as he descended the concrete stairs to the walkway that ran alongside the aging two-story house. The flat cream paint on the door frame was starting to peel, revealing spots of bright yellow enamel underneath. They must be either P.I.s hired by the Guardsmen's Office or they're Guardsmen themselves. Probably P.I.s, judging from the cigarette. Real Thanatologists don't smoke.

Rick folded his umbrella and set it down while he fumbled for his key. When he put it into the lock, his hands were trembling. Inside, the suite smelled moldy and damp, as usual. He tossed his coat on the kitchen table and let himself sink down into the ageing armchair in the main room. But as soon as he sat down, he noticed the light blinking on his answering machine. Blink, blink, blink. Three messages.

After the tape rewound, he heard a firm female voice. Linda from the Guardsmen's Office. "Rick, we know you're there. Did you think you could blow and we wouldn't find you? You know better than that. We've put out an Oppressive Person proclaim on you, Rick. You're an O.P. You know what that means." *Beep.*

89

Rick knew what that meant.

Linda again. "Rick, we know you copied files before you blew. You've got to give those back. Those are copyrighted materials. They belong to the Guardsman's Office. Remember, everything belongs to TFS." *Beep.*

An old Thanatology slogan. Everything belongs to TFS – T. Frank Sheppard. The author of a series of dungeons-and-dragons fantasy novels who had spun his fantasies into a New Age religion. A religion that he, Rick Saunders, had followed for seven years, even rising to the rank of Colonel in the Guardsmen.

The next voice was familiar. Rick had left a message on his voicemail a few hours before. "Mr. Saunders, this is Damian Lawson with the Vancouver *Province.* You left a message about having some information on the Church of Thanatology? You said you could show me some of those files they keep on former members. I'm very interested. If you want to call me in the evening you can reach me at home." Then he gave his home number. *Beep.*

Rick considered erasing the tape and not calling back, but he stopped and jotted down the number. Did he dare call?

The idea to leave had come over him suddenly. One day he knew he couldn't take it any more. The games of intimidation he had to play with members who had left, or were wavering. The files he kept on everyone, their stats, what courses they had taken and what level they had risen to. The people he had sent to RPC – Re-education Program Corps – as a form of punishment, and the time that he himself was sent to RPC when his stats were poor for a month. That time, they'd busted his rank to sergeant and ordered him to clean the floor of the Guardsman's Office every day for two weeks with a toothbrush.

But if he called Lawson, the intimidation would get worse. They'd call his employer, say he was crazy or a drug addict. They'd tell Lawson the same things. They'd broadcast it far and wide that this Rick Saunders who was saying bad things about the Church of Thanatology was really just a lonely, pathetic, mentally unstable loser.

And then the lawsuits would start. They'd sue him even if they had no chance of winning. They'd sue him just because it would cost him time and money to get the lawsuits dismissed. They would do everything in their power to destroy him, because now he'd been proclaimed an OP, and an OP was fair game.

Suddenly Rick remembered a face – a haggard, intense face begging Rick to leave him alone. Pondrachuk. Peter Pondrachuk, the last OP to which Rick had been assigned. He'd known Peter slightly; they'd taken some courses together when they were both new to Thanatology. One time their mentor assigned them the task of staring into each other's eyes for an hour without blinking. They weren't supposed to say anything or do anything, just stare. It was supposed to clear your blockages so the evaluator could tell you what your problems were. They made it about half way before Peter couldn't help looking away. He laughed and shrugged when he did it. "You got me, Rick," he said. "You're one tough dude, I'll tell you that." Peter was a good guy – for a while there, at the beginning, they'd almost been friends. Then he blew. That was bad enough, but he made it worse when he started talking to this reporter, this Lawson guy from the *Province*. So the word came down to the Guardsmen's Office: Get Pondrachuk.

Rick found him hiding out in Surrey, in his stepfather's basement suite. For two weeks Rick and Linda Harper, both trusted Guardsmen who often worked together, kept watch in the street outside his house. During the long boring hours when nothing much was happening, they played games like "I Spy" just to stay awake. Or one of them would read aloud from a T. Frank Sheppard novel or a Thanatology text while the other kept watch. Linda even told jokes sometimes – she had a whole routine, and her timing was dead on. Rick's sides ached from laughing. But whenever Peter came out of the house, they zipped their lips and got down to business.

As soon as Peter appeared, Rick or Linda would get out of the car and start taking snapshots. Or they would follow behind him, videotaping him as he walked down the street. That was all. They weren't supposed to touch him, just scare him.

Peter was easy to scare. By the end of two weeks he was a wreck. He stopped going to work and just hid out in his suite. Every so often they'd see the curtains part on his basement window, and might just glimpse the light glinting off his spectacles.

He knew they were out there, and that made him afraid to even come out. When he finally did, he looked like he hadn't showered for a week. He shambled over to their car, though he stopped several times on the way and looked down abstractedly before continuing. Arriving at the driver's side window, he only glanced at Rick once, with a shock of recognition. Then he looked away.

"Please." He flapped his hands wildly as if shooing away insects. "Please – just go away. I won't talk to that reporter anymore. Please leave me alone. Please."

Rick could hardly look at him. Linda leaned across him from the passenger's seat and spoke up. "You're not going to say anything more to anyone about Thanatology, am I right, Peter?"

He took one brief, frightened look in Linda's direction, then looked away again.

"If you do, we'll come back."

"I ... won't ... say anything," Peter mumbled.

While they were driving back to the Guardsmen's Office, Linda kept looking over at Rick sharply. He knew she was upset with him for not speaking up to Peter. Finally she came out with it.

"You got a problem handling OPs, Rick?" He knew he was in trouble then. Linda would report him and he might end up on RPC, or worse. They might bust him down to buck private or order him to repeat all his courses, which means he'd have to pay for them again. Two days later he blew.

Rick stood up and hauled his wooden kitchen chair over to one of the small rectangular windows through which light from the street trickled into his basement suite. By standing on the chair he could just see the street and the rain slanting down in the glow of the streetlight. The P.I.s were still there. One of them was still smoking; he could see the faint glow on the driver's side. They were undoubtedly bored – their purpose was just to send him a message, a warning. Should he go and confront them? But if he did, what would he say?

Let them stew, he decided. Rick got down off the chair and returned it to the kitchen. He opened the fridge and peered in, looking for a beer. One left. No sooner had he popped the tab when the phone rang.

"Rick, is everything all right?" It was Sally, his sister in North Van.

"Yes, I'm fine. Why, what's up?"

"There were some strange guys here this afternoon asking questions. They didn't look like Thanatologists. They were just sort of creepy. I told them I didn't know where you live."

"They were P.I.s, probably. Don't worry, they're not going to do anything. They're just trying to send a message."

"Listen, Rick. Maybe you should get out of Vancouver. Why don't you go back to Hundred Mile House or something."

"Go back and live with Mom and Dad? At my age?"

"Well, you've got to do something. I'm scared, Rick. I don't want to have any more strange guys coming around here when Andrew's at work. And what about you? Have they found you yet?"

Rick pressed the cold beer can to his forehead to help him think. He didn't want to frighten Sally any further. Should he tell her? Things were only going to get worse if he called Lawson. "Yeah, they found me. About a week ago."

Sally was silent for a moment. "Well, just – just – don't take any – I'm – I just want you to be careful, okay? We all need you, Rick. Bobby says you're his favorite uncle."

Rick snorted, but felt pleased. "That's not saying much, since Andrew's brothers all live in Toronto. I have an unfair advantage."

"Rick, you know what I mean! He adores you. You take care of yourself."

They rang off. Rick thought about how he used to amuse his nephew on his visits, even when he was a Guardsman. While Sally was making dinner and Andrew was whipping up his special salad, Rick would be in the driveway with Bobby, pretending to be a goalie while the boy lobbed tennis balls at him with his hockey stick. Rick stopped a few but he always let enough go by that Bobby could feel he was NHL material. During those visits Rick felt relief, as if for once he could put aside the strident intensity of his life as a Guardsman and be himself again.

Rick finished the beer in three quick gulps. Then he dragged the chair over to the window again to take another look. Still there. That settled it. If he didn't stand up to the Church of Thanatology now, who was going to make sure that Bobby didn't end up going through the same thing in twenty years time?

Crossing over to the phone, he picked up the slip of paper with the reporter's phone number on it, and noticed that his hand was shaking a little. "O.K., Mr. Lawson," he muttered aloud, gulping back his nervousness as he dialed. "Let's play ball."

Fake It 'Til You Make It

YOU WAIT FOR FRANK TO CALL. While you wait, you pace back and forth in your kitchen with half an ear tuned to the reedy voice of Ted Jones on a tape recorder. If you don't leave pronto, you'll be late for work. Yet you can't leave, because you need to talk to Frank about whether you're going with him to the sales convention in L.A. You can't make up your mind. Come on, Frank, hurry up.

Ted Jones is posing hypothetical situations. "Nothing much would happen if all the lawyers disappeared tomorrow. If all the doctors vanished, what do you think would happen? I'll tell you what would happen: Nothing. The world would go on pretty much like before. But what if all the salesmen in the world disappeared overnight? The whole economy would come to a halt. Everything would stop!"

Your perambulations take you past the refrigerator, stove, and kitchen cupboards, and out into the dining area where you glance at your IKEA white table and single chair, and finally lead you to the dining room window with its view of a parking lot. Your return journey permits you to review these domestic objects in reverse order: table, cupboards, stove, refrigerator.

Each time you pass the refrigerator, you can't avoid seeing the VISA bill with its large unpaid balance affixed to the freezer compartment with a magnet shaped like the state of Kansas. The sight of the bill brings a wave of chagrin, but this is quickly followed by a feeling of relief: at least you ran up these debts for yourself and for your own needs.

This thought always brings with it a renewal of the vow you once made to yourself: never again will you blindly follow others, wasting years of your life as you once did. For several years, you had lost sight of your career because you foolishly devoted yourself to enriching a soft-spoken Indian guru. It was a bitter lesson you are determined to never repeat. From now on, you will be your own boss and decide your own future. You will forge your own destiny.

You are determined to bury the memory of the many years you wasted as an acolyte of Celestial Meditation, or "CM." You even spent five years at the Maharajah University in the middle of Kansas, learning to be a "mantra flyer" – one of those select few who levitated through mental powers alone. According to the Maharajah, the more mantra flyers there were, the more positive energy there would be to elevate the world.

In those days, you rose early every morning and walked to a large illuminated bubble dome which, in the half light of dawn, looked like nothing so much as a giant, glowing UFO plunked down in the middle of a Kansas corn field. There, you sat cross-legged on the rubber floor mat, and at some point during your meditation, you hopped – briefly – off the mat, perhaps once or maybe a few times. But was it only your desperate desire to do something – anything – that allowed you to fly?

In any case, what does it matter now?

When you finally quit CM, you had no money. Your only option was to return to your parents' home until you could get back on your feet. You had learned precious few job skills during your years following the Maharajah, so you took casual laboring jobs until one of them turned into a steady job at a warehouse. It wasn't very exciting, and it didn't pay very well, but at least it was work. Eventually you saved enough money to move into your own apartment. Still, when you sit on your inflatable sofa in front of your television after another dreary work day, you can't help wondering – is this it? There are days, frankly, when you miss the Maharajah University and your friends in CM.

But then you discover Vitalidrink. One dreary winter Saturday as you trudge through the snow to your local coffee shop, you spot a hand-lettered sign taped to a street lamp. In large red letters it proclaims: "EARN $300 TO $500 PER WEEK IN YOUR SPARE TIME." Underneath these words dangle several strips of paper bearing a phone number and the name "Frank." At those rates your can more than double your salary. You pull off one of the strips and shove it into your shirt pocket. Back home, your make the call.

"I saw your sign. What sort of work are you talking about?"

"We're not talking nickels and dimes here. We're talking serious cash. Mounds of moolah. If you work hard, before long you'll be rolling in dough."

"But what is it, exactly?" you ask.

"It's called Vitalidrink. A new health drink that's just catching on. You get everything you need for good health in a single drink. Hardly any calories, so you'll lose weight, too. But listen. Why don't you come to our meeting on Saturday?"

The Vitalidrink people have a room at the Holiday Inn where they meet on Saturday mornings to spread the good news about the health benefits and financial miracles available through Vitalidrink. You are informed that if you mix this marvelous scientifically-formulated protein powder with milk or juice twice daily, and also take all the vitamin and mineral supplements included in the program, you will not only lose weight, but could earn a huge income by turning others onto the product.

You can't deny you need to lose weight. Yet even more appealing is the large potential income you could have as a Vitalidrink distributor. It all seems too good to be true. You sign on.

At first it is a challenge to eat only one solid meal a day. You replace these with a long, cool glass of Vitalidrink and a handful of vitamins. But as time goes on, you begin to enjoy the feeling of self-discipline it gives you, and you even begin to like the silty taste of the Vitalidrink powder mixed with orange juice or milk. Your pounds melt away. Your hunger pangs gradually subside and you feel more energy, as promised. Within months you are as slim as you've ever been.

The other part of the Vitalidrink System, however – the part about finding "downline" distributors to generate royalties – hasn't worked out quite so well. When you signed on, Frank advised you to bring your family and friends into the Vitalidrink System. But your dad laughed at your sales pitch. Your mom said, "That looks interesting, dear," and promised to try the drink, but doesn't want to sell the products herself. Your sister said she'd think about it, and didn't.

Finally you take your old high school buddy, Lanny, to the Vitalidrink distributor meeting. "Cool," Lanny says when the slide show introduction ends. He pokes you in the belly. "You were starting to look kind of porky anyway. Too much sitting around levitating."

You try to convince Lanny that he'll earn a pile of money if he signs up. But he only shrugs. "I don't know, old buddy. Me and Sandra are doing pretty good the way we are. I'm not into this salesman thing." Then he grins – that old wicked grin you remember from afternoons spent hanging out behind the high school. "Maybe if they made Viagra or something. You know, like a herbal version or whatever."

You turn to recruiting people you don't know. You put out signs modeled after Frank's, as well as other signs proclaiming "NEED 20-30 PEOPLE TO TRY NEW WEIGHT LOSS SYSTEM," but you only find a handful of people willing to try the products. "You're just not doing the System properly," Frank insists, so you apply yourself to following the Vitalidrink System to the letter.

As part of the System, the first thing you do when you get up is put on a cassette tape of the inspiring speeches of Vitalidrink founder, Ted Jones. You listen to Ted attentively while showering, dressing, and throwing Vitalidrink and milk into your blender. Jones – now a multi-millionaire – started out by selling his miracle powder out of the trunk of his car. Only over time had he worked out the details of his amazing new System, which one day will transform the entire world, making everyone rich and slim.

Yet following the System involves far more than listening to Jones. You wear a metal button everywhere you go. "BE FAT FREE. JUST ASK ME!" You learn to shrug off the sarcastic jibes of your co workers at the warehouse. You plaster a bumper sticker with the same words on your car with your phone number written underneath in felt pen.

And then there's the advertising. You print up a thousand flyers with your phone number on them, promising, "EARN $300 TO $500 PER WEEK IN YOUR SPARE TIME!" and put them in mailboxes or slide them under apartment doors. You get lots of phone calls, but few callers actually come to a meeting. What's left to try?

At one point you seriously consider quitting your job so you can devote more time to the System, but Frank discourages the idea. "Just follow the System, and success is bound to come." Once again, Frank recites the fabled story of Blair Dumphries, who had been a humble grass-cutter out on the west coast until he discovered the miracle of Vitalidrink. Now, he's pulling down six figures per annum. You take Frank's advice. You keep your boring job, though increasingly you find yourself chafing at the juvenile antics of your co workers, who talk about nothing but sports, sex and beer – or sex, sports and beer – depending on the season.

"Maybe you need to go to a sales convention," Frank suggests. "There's one in Los Angeles next month. You could go if you make supervisor." But making supervisor would require you to achieve an impossible volume of sales. You give up the idea. Then Frank, a natural salesman, volunteers to transfer a large number of his own sales points to you so you can go. But will you?

You stop pacing as you consider your options. Certainly if you are going to make it big in this business, you need to become a supervisor and attend these conventions. Many times you've daydreamed of swaggering into the warehouse office, grinning, with your pants stuffed with green, and telling your stunned boss where he can stick his stupid job. But Frank keeps urging you to keep your job until you're really raking in the bucks.

You resume pacing, but once again the VISA bill catches your eye. If you need a good reason not to go, this is it. You've already stretched your credit further than you like just to get this far in the business. Flying to L.A. and staying at a hotel would be another hefty hit. Unless your income rises substantially, you can't possibly pay it off in less than a year. You know you should tell Frank, "Enough is enough!" and dig in your heels. But if you do that, you might never see the miraculous wealth lying just ahead, if only you were to persist just a little bit longer, or invest just a little bit more.

On the other hand, if you go to the sales convention, you can see and hear Jones in person. That alone might bring a huge boost in sales. Frank promises as much. "After my first convention, my sales just exploded!"

Back and forth, back and forth, you pace, while listening to Jones carrying on with his pep talk. He's just getting to the part where he advises struggling distributors to "follow the System and see what happens." A person who fails to lose weight on the Vitalidrink plan must be "cheating"; similarly, Jones reasons, a distributor who isn't making money is probably "cheating" by not following the System to the letter.

Someone in Jones' audience asks him a question. What about distributors who haven't made it yet, but who need to convince their downline they have? "That's when you've gotta fake it 'til you make it!" Jones roars.

The phone rings. Decision time.

"Whattya say, buddy?" Frank yells in his usual super-cheerful tone. "Are you coming to L.A.?"

You think about your job in an industrial park, and the dull routine of stacking and moving boxes, day after day. Then you think about Blair Dumphries, his jeans covered with grass stains, looking up from his lawn mower, and stopping a passer-by to ask about a metal button.

"Hey, sure, Frank. I'm in! I'll book the ticket today." Frank vows that your sales will "go through the roof!," and then hangs up quickly.

As you leave, you feel your uncertainty melting away. What a great feeling to no longer be a follower. Finally, you are your own boss.

Living Water

WE CAN HEAR THEM all the way down the hall, even though our door's closed and they think we're asleep.

"Hear that? They're arguing," I whisper to Donny, whose bed is across from mine. Model airplanes, suspended by threads tacked to the ceiling, hang over his bed. He turns over to face me. A little moonlight comes through the window so I can see just half his face. I'm seven and he's nine.

"Not arguing. Just talking. They're scared."

"Scared? But Dad *never* gets scared. He was in the war and everything!"

"That's different. They're scared all right. You heard what they talked about at supper."

"You mean about the missiles? And what the American President said on T.V.?"

"Yeah, all that stuff about Cuba and how maybe there's going to be a war."

"Aw, I bet *Dad*'s not scared."

"So go find out for yourself."

"They'll quit talking if I go down there."

"Just sneak down the hall and hide around the corner so they don't know you're there."

I put on my pajamas (which I always take off as soon as Mom leaves because I don't like them) and open the door. I have to be careful because our bedroom door creaks. I tiptoe down the hall and stop just before I get there. The hallway's dark but there's lots of light coming from the kitchen. I can hear Mom talking when I get close. Her voice is shaking.

"Dear Lord, please watch over Canada, and our city of Calgary, and especially keep our family safe in this time of danger. Please guide President Kennedy and Premier Khrushchev so there won't be a war. And please guide Prime Minister Diefenbaker, so he'll know what to do."

"Oh yes, please, God!"

That's my Dad. But he *never* prays! In fact, he hardly ever goes to St. Andrew's with the rest of us.

I peek around the corner. Dad's sitting at the kitchen table with his back to me, his head bowed in prayer. He has a great broad back and a large head of thick black hair. He's holding Mom's hands. She's looking down, still speaking to God with her eyes closed. She has curly red hair around a plump, freckled face. She's very pretty, and she has this lovely accent which she says is because she's a "Yorkshire lass."

"And, Lord, no matter what happens, please watch over our four children – Donny, Glenn, Rita, and Shelley – and don't let them be hurt. They're just innocent kids, Lord. Please keep them safe!" Mom sounds like she's crying.

"Yes, *please*, God!"

I must have made a noise. They look around and see me there, and right away they drop their linked hands.

"Hey, sport! You're supposed to be in bed!" Dad wipes something from his eyes when he glances over at me.

"Come here, Glenny," Mom says, holding out her arms. I don't care that I'm too old to sit in her big, soft lap or to be called "Glenny." I just want her to hug me right now. I run over and jump on her lap and she lets out a little gasp. She has a cup of tea in front of her. So does Dad. "How come you're up, Glenn? Can't you sleep, honey?"

"I need a glass of water."

Dad goes over to the sink. He takes down a plastic tumbler and fills it and brings it over to me.

"For your *majesty*," he says, placing it in front of me with a low bow, pretending to take off his cap. He's holding back a smile, and I laugh. I love my Dad. He's always doing things like that, sort of making fun but you know he doesn't mean it. Mom kisses me on the side of my head.

I take a few sips and then set it down. I look over at Dad, who's sitting down again across from me. He's my hero. He once flew a bomber back to England from Germany with one engine shot out and half of his crew wounded. They gave him a medal for that.

"Dad, you know back when you were in the war? Did you ever get scared?"

He looks at me for a long time before he says anything. "Sure, I was, Glenn. Sure, I was. But you don't think about it. You just put it away and you keep on going." He gets up from the table and starts pacing around.

That's what always happens whenever we ask him about the war. He doesn't like to talk about it, so whenever we ask, it makes him upset.

Mom gives me a squeeze and then shifts her body so I have to get down.

"Come along, honey, I'll put you to bed again, now you've had your water." We walk back towards the hallway. At the last moment I look back and see Dad looking out the window into the night. He seems far away.

"So was he scared?" Donny whispers after Mom closes the door.

"Yeah. Mom, too."

"See? Told ya!"

I think that was the last time I saw Dad looking that way, like he had no idea what to do.

❧❧❧

A few weeks later it's getting cold and Mom and Dad take us to the North Hill Shopping Centre to buy winter coats and boots. After we're finished at Simpson-Sears, we start walking past the Dominion Foods store and that's when we see this big brown hut, with its door propped open, sitting right in the middle of the mall. There's a guy in a suit holding out pamphlets, and when we get closer, we find out the hut is actually a bomb shelter, and the man's telling people how you have to bury this thing in your back yard. Then if the Russians start a war, you get inside and close the door and you're safe.

We look the hut all over and Donny and I both think it's pretty neat. Dad says we can't afford one, and anyway our house is rented, so we can't go putting something like that in our back yard.

103

But just when we're starting to walk away, this other guy walks up and speaks to my Dad. He's our neighbor who lives across the road from us. We don't really know him, except Mom once told me he's the minister of a small church down the street from St. Andrew's.

"Do you think a bomb shelter would protect you and your family on the Day of Judgment, neighbor?" the minister asks Dad.

Dad shrugs, and waves at the hut. "Well, no, but it might come in handy if the Russians drop the bomb."

"And if they drop the bomb, wouldn't that be the End of Days anyway?"

"Well, maybe not the end, but just about." Dad looks uncomfortable. He wants to keep walking.

"And what will you do when that day comes? Crawl under a table and pray? Or will you be among those the Lord takes with him to His Heavenly Kingdom?"

"Listen, I can't talk right now. My family's here and we've got shopping to do. But I know you live on my street, so if you want to come around some time, I'll gladly hear you out. If you want to talk to me you'll have to come over in the evening or on a Saturday afternoon. I've gotta tell you, that whole Cuban thing really made me think. I wasn't a praying man before then, but now I've sort of changed. I wouldn't mind hearing what you've got to say, uh, Pastor ... ."

"Pastor Divine. Why don't you attend one of my services at the Living Water Pentecostal Church? We're close to the Anglican church, which I believe your wife attends." The minister hands my Dad a brochure, which he puts next to the one from the bomb shelter guy.

"Sure, maybe. We could visit there some Sunday." Dad walks away, sticking the brochures in his pocket before grabbing Rita's hand. We leave and start walking in the direction of the hobby shop. This gets Donny and me excited, because Donny likes to look at model airplanes, and I like to look at model ships. But while we're walking away, Dad looks back and sees the Pastor watching him, and they give each other a little wave.

Pastor Divine isn't tall, so his pulpit is shorter than the ones they have at St. Andrew's. But he talks louder and longer than any of the ministers at St. Andrew's. While he's talking he leans over the pulpit, like he's trying to see what we're thinking, and he stares at each of us, one after the other, to make sure we're listening. His head is bald but he has a large ring of wavy grey hair around the sides. When he talks, his big bushy eyebrows go up and down and he keeps pointing at things like his Bible, or upwards at God.

"Behold, for the Day of the Lord is at hand. He is coming on the clouds of heaven to gather his believers, who will sit with him on the right hand of the Father in Heaven. Be vigilant and prepare yourself, for the time may come at any moment, lest ye be caught unawares. Beware especially of the apostate churches that lull you with sweet words and easy burdens. The Lord expects much more of you than to visit His house once a week and sing a few songs."

Here he looks over at my Mom. She sees him doing it, too, because she blushes until her face is almost as red as her hair. Then Pastor Divine looks away and goes on talking. After a while Mom's face goes back to its normal color, but I can tell she's still mad.

When we get out of Pastor Divine's church, it's a lot later than when we usually get out of St. Andrew's, and I'm hungry. Dad's walking towards the car, with Donny and me following. "Well, I don't think I'll be going *there* again," Mom says, holding Shelley in her left arm and tugging Rita's hand with her right. Dad turns.

"Maybe you won't go, Marge, but *I* will. I think this man is really onto something. What he said about the Last Days and all. It's too important."

"You can come here if you want, but the kids and I are staying with St. Andrew's," Mom says, stopping short and almost causing Rita to tumble onto her knees. Mom and Dad glare at each other for a while.

Dad finally shrugs and starts walking to the car again. "Oh well, they're pretty close to each other, we can do it all in one trip."

After that, Dad goes to the Living Water church, and the rest of us go to St. Andrew's with Mom. Mom always packs a picnic lunch of sandwiches and orange drink because we have to wait a long time in the car before Dad gets out of his service.

But more and more, I hear them arguing at night, after we've gone to bed. Dad says the pastor told him that he's "unevenly yoked" because his wife isn't a strong believer. Dad keeps trying to get Mom to switch to the Living Water church, but she always says no. Sometimes when we're in bed we hear them arguing, and then it takes me a long time to fall asleep.

In early July, when the ice is long gone from the rivers and the spring runoff has slowed, Pastor Divine decides it's time to baptize all the new church members like my Dad. He does it the way they did it in the Bible, with people ducking under the water and everything, so he tells the church members to come to Calgary's Stanley Park on a Saturday evening so the new members can be baptized in the gentle Elbow River. It's a combined baptism and church picnic, so we're all excited to go, though Mom doesn't look too happy. But she packs a basket full of hot dogs and potato salad anyway and comes along.

When we get there, we find a lot of other people Dad knows standing around talking. They've taken over several picnic tables and barbecue pits and there are some kids splashing in the river. But when Pastor Divine arrives the kids get out of the water and we all stand around and listen to him talk. Since it's Stampede week, he's dressed up like a cowboy in blue jeans with a checked shirt and a little string tie. He's even got a black cowboy hat on, pulled down to cover his bald head. He tells us that baptism is a promise to God and Jesus to be loyal for the rest of your life, and he reads the part in the Bible where Jesus goes to John the Baptist to be baptized in the Jordan, and John tells Jesus he isn't fit to tie his shoes, and Jesus tells him to go ahead anyway. Then he walks down to the Elbow River and walks right out into the water until it's up to his chest, and he starts calling out the names of the people to be baptized. When he says "Russell Maddox," my Dad gets up from the picnic table where we're sitting, and he walks straight down to Pastor Divine and gets in the water with all his clothes on, never looking back. The sun is shining into our eyes so all I can see of Dad is his silhouette. Then Pastor Divine says a few words, and suddenly grabs my Dad's hair and plunges his head under the water, and then pulls it up, and for a moment my Dad is bent over, like he's spitting up water. Then he turns around and starts walking back in our direction, and the setting sun makes his whole outline glow while he walks toward us.

When he gets to the table Mom asks him, "How was that?"

"Wonderful," he says, still dripping with water. "Like the Holy Spirit is inside me now."

"Well, so long as that's the only kind of spirits inside you, that's fine with me." She turns to open up the picnic cooler and starts taking out the hot dogs and marshmallows and stuff. "Can we have our picnic now? The kids are starving."

"Sure. I'll start the fire. When the baptisms are finished, the kids can go swimming." He turns to the metal barbecue and dumps the coals in, squirts on the starter fluid, and starts the fire. I come over to watch. Once the fire's going, I ask, "What does if feel like to have the Holy Spirit inside you, Dad?"

"I can't describe it, Glenn." He shrugs as he flips some hot dogs over on the grill. "When you're old enough, you'll find out for yourself."

"But is it a good feeling, like now you're really strong and you'll never be afraid?"

"No, it's more like I'm committed now. I've got to do what the Lord wants. It's like when I joined the air force. The very first rule was that you had to follow the Wing Commander. Jesus is my Wing Commander now, Glenn."

"More like Pastor Divine is your Wing Commander, Russell," Mom puts in from over at the picnic table, where she's setting out the potato salad. "He's got you wrapped around his little finger, and you can't even see it." Dad drops his barbecue fork and turns to Mom.

"Marge, don't say those things. Let's not spoil the picnic."

I walk away because I don't want to hear them arguing. When the hot dogs are ready I get mine and go down to the river bank to eat it while I poke a stick into the weeds along the edge. Later the church people announce egg-and-spoon races and sack races and three-legged races. Donny and I tie our legs together and we come in second in the boys' race. Some men set up a horseshoe stake and start throwing horseshoes while their wives talk. The sun has almost set now and it's just that perfect time on a summer evening when everybody's warm and content and there's nothing much moving except a few mosquitoes. But when I look back to the picnic table, my Mom and Dad are still arguing. That's when I start to wonder if they might split up.

But I start feeling a lot more hope a week later when I overhear Dad and Mom deciding to take us all for a holiday to Pigeon Lake – way up by Edmonton – so we can "pull together as a family." Mom makes him promise he won't talk about his church or Pastor Divine the whole time we're away. We'll just go away for one week, and we'll have fun, and we'll never argue, not even once, she tells him. Okay, he says.

ｅｊｅｊｅｊ

Dad drives all day on the Number 2 Highway to Edmonton until we turn onto another road to Wetaskiwin. When we see the sign for "Ma Me O Beach" we all perk up. Pretty soon we drive right into the town of Pigeon Lake and Dad stops to talk to somebody about renting a beach cabin. He comes back jangling a set of keys in front of him and everyone cheers. When we get to the cottage, we see it's a small place made of pine logs and wood smoke and pure hot summer.

Mom carries the food hamper inside. Dad makes Donny and me stop running so we can carry things. Rita and Shelley are too young so he lets them run around and play. The first thing Dad takes out of the car is the Bible and the other books Pastor Divine told him to take.

"Oh, Russell, remember what we decided. Why don't you leave those books in the car?"

"The pastor said this is the perfect place to study the Word. No distractions. Don't worry, I'm not going to say anything."

Mom sighs. "We just drove nearly two hundred miles. And now you're going to spend your whole time reading? We might as well stay home."

"Nothing's stopping you and the kids from having fun. What's the problem?"

The cabin has oil lamps and a wood stove and bunk beds. But if you have to go to the bathroom you've got to go to this smelly

108

little house out back that has a hole cut in the bench. But nobody minds, because we're all too excited. Donny doesn't even get mad when I claim the top bunk.

By the time we're all unpacked, Dad's sitting at the kitchen table, next to the oil lamp, reading. Mom looks over at him while she makes supper, but doesn't say anything. Dad made a fire for her in the wood stove and Mom's boiling spaghetti. Shelley's sleeping on a pile of blankets on the floor and Rita's coloring in her book. Donny's reading a Superman comic book and I'm looking up at the ceiling from my top bunk. I keep closing one eye and then the other to see how different things look if you use only one eye. There are faces in the wood grain on the rafters but they don't scare me. They have weird round eyes and mouths surrounded by wavy rings that keep going out and out until they turn into shapeless things, like ghosts.

"Pastor Divine's right," Dad finally says, and Mom looks over at him from the stove. I peer down at them from the top bunk. I have a pretty good view from where I'm lying. I can see both of them and the table where Dad's sitting with the stove behind it. Dad lifts up the Bible and holds it towards Mom and then points at a page in the other book. "These are the Last Days. It says right here there's going to be 'wars and rumors of war' right before the end, and you know we just went through that whole Cuban thing."

Mom drops the spoon in the water and waves her hands at Dad, like she's shooing away a dog. "Oh, Russell, hush. That Cuban crisis was last year and we're all still here. Don't talk that way. Remember, you promised."

"The kids might as well get used to it. Pastor Divine says we've got to get ready, because the Lord's coming on the clouds of heaven."

"Well, if he drops by tonight, I'll give him a big kiss, and cut him a nice big piece of pie." Mom brought a lemon meringue pie up from the city for our dessert. She's not looking at Dad. When she says something like that she pretends to be serious, but if I was close enough, I'd see a little smile on her face all the same. She rescues her spoon by using a knife to raise the handle out of the boiling water.

"It doesn't work that way. We're all going to be lifted up into the air. It'll be the Rapture and everybody'll be flying."

"Fine by me. Better view."

I try to imagine what it would be like to fly through the air to meet the powerful Jesus that Dad talks about. Will the clouds feel all cool and wet when we shoot right through them? Will Jesus be big and bearded and shiny and have a whole bunch of golden rays coming out of his head like in Dad's pictures?

Mom takes the pot off the stove and carries it to the back door. She dumps the hot water on the ground but holds the lid so the spaghetti won't fall out. Then she dumps the noodles into a blue plastic bowl and calls. "Supper time!"

I climb down off the upper bunk by stepping on Donny's bunk. He's already up. We all scramble to the table while Mom takes the pot full of sauce from the stove and pours it over the spaghetti. Then she wakes up Shelley and carries her over to the table. Dad puts his Bible away for once, and pretty soon we start laughing about stuff and everything feels like the way it used to be.

❧❧❧

I'm going to make the biggest sand castle in the world. It'll have moats and canals and all these flags on top and drawbridges and places where you can drive trucks into it and everything.

Donny's not interested in helping, though. He spends all his time swimming. He says he's going to swim out to those buoys that are strung out along a rope to separate the swimming area from the boating part, and then he's going to swim back again.

I like playing in the sand better. I started building my castle today. I just have a pail and a shovel, but I've already got the corners marked out and I started on the walls in between. Shelley helps me. She's only two, but I taught her how to pat the sand down after I scoop it into the shape of a wall. Donny and Rita would rather swim. They're water people, but me and Shelley are sand people, that's what I figure.

Mom worries about Donny trying to swim out so far but Dad thinks he's got the right idea. During the afternoon he puts down his books and comes over to watch what I'm doing and then he tells me, "Jesus warned people not to build their houses upon sand. If a storm comes, it'll be washed away and everything will be lost."

I don't get what he means. I'm not building a house, I'm making a sand castle. Then he points to Donny and says, "Why don't you go swimming like your brother? The water will do you good. Jesus talked about the living water: once you drink it, you'll never thirst again. Jump in and drink the water of life. That's what Pastor Divine told me when he baptized me. Go on, get out there. Start swimming like your brother."

Mom comes over and says, "Why don't you let Glenny be? He's been building his sand castle all day and that's what he likes to do. At least we don't have to worry about him drowning."

But Dad says, "Glenn's gotta learn to be a man. He should be out there swimming like Donny. Come on, now, scoot!" He jerks his head in the direction of the lake. So I get up, leaving my pail and shovel, and go down to the edge of the lake. "Jump, Glenn!" Dad yells, and I step into the water. It's cold. Then I slowly walk out until I feel like I can bear to stick my head under. I splash around for a while, but then I feel some black squishy things on my arms and legs biting me. I run out.

"Don't be scared honey, they're just leeches," Mom says as she lights matches to burn them off. Four of them! They fall onto the sand and I step on them. The one on my right hand left a diamond-shaped mark on my palm in the place where it sucked my blood. It felt like I was being pricked all over but as soon as the leeches came off the feeling stopped. "Go back to your sand castle. I'll tell Daddy you've had enough swimming."

Donny comes over and tells me that he always swims far out really fast so the leeches can't catch him. I say I don't believe him, so he tells me he got one on his arm once, but he wasn't scared and he just pulled it off.

Later Dad comes over and watches me for a while. "Sorry I made you swim, Glenn. You do what you want. Sometimes I forget I don't know everything." He watches me for a while and says, "Maybe you'll be an engineer when you grow up. Build a whole bunch of skyscrapers or something." That makes me feel great. It's like I have my old Dad back, the way he was before

Pastor Divine. After a while he walks away and goes back to reading. I keep on building my sand castle.

❧❧❧

It's Tuesday, cool and cloudy, and the rain is falling a little, so it's not much fun. But I'd rather be on the beach than indoors. Mom says that if it really starts to rain we'll have to go back and play card games. I hope it doesn't rain so much that it washes away my castle. It's pretty big now and I've made a second set of walls inside the first.

After dinner Mom decides it's too rainy to go back to the beach, so we stay in and play cards. I really like the smell of the wood burning and I like the way the oil lamps make neat shadows on the walls. Mom teaches us Hearts. We sort of get it, except Shelley, of course. She just watches. Mom helps Rita a lot. It's fun, though Dad doesn't join in. He's in a corner reading again, but Mom looks over at him anyway.

"Won't you join us, dear? It's not too late."

"Pastor Divine doesn't approve of card games. If you were a believer, you wouldn't be doing that."

"Goodness, it's just Hearts, dear. It's not like we're playing poker or anything." After that Mom only talks to us, and doesn't look at Dad.

❧❧❧

The rain's still coming down this morning so we're not going to the beach until it stops. I wonder if my castle's still standing. I'll probably have to start over. But I found this book somebody left behind in the cabin and it has all these little cartoons and crossword puzzles, so I'm sitting at the table trying to do them.

"Mom, can I go to the store and get another comic book? I'm bored!" Donny says. When we first drove in, we saw a store with a sign saying "Lee's Confectionery."

"Me too! I want to go too!" I shout. I want a grape Popsicle.

"Boys, you'll have to wait until after lunch. If the rain stops, maybe we can go," Mom says.

"Aw, Mom!"

Dad looks up from his book. "I can take them," he says.

"Yea-a-ah!" we all say. Rita joins in, too.

"What for? We've got all we need."

"I need to make a phone call."

"What, to Pastor Divine? Can't it wait?"

"It's important. Don't nag, Marge. A Christian wife should support her husband." He says this loudly, the way he does when he's repeating things they say at his church.

"'A Christian wife,'" Mom says with scorn. "You're imitating him now! Remember, we promised we wouldn't talk about that."

"You're the one who's talking about it, not me." Dad turns to us and pulls out the car keys and jingles them. "Coming, kids?"

We all jump up and put on our shoes and coats. Mom shrugs and gets out Shelley's outdoor stuff and puts it on her. "Well, I might as well come along. Maybe I'll see something we need."

At the store Mom sets Shelley down on the counter and lets us roam around while she talks to the Chinese people who run the store. They're old and wrinkly but the store lady likes Shelley, so she gives her a red Halloween sucker. Mom tells the lady we drove up from Calgary. She asks her if she has any kids.

"All grown up. Going to school in Edmonton." The Chinese lady reaches under the counter and pulls out a picture of her kids. The Chinese man, who's been watching Donny and me to make sure we don't steal anything, looks over at the picture too.

"Two boys, two girls, just like you!" he says, handing the photo to Mom.

"Youngest girl is coming next month," the store lady says excitedly. "If you here, you see her."

"We're only here for a week. Maybe next year," Mom says, but she glances at the picture. Mostly, though, she's keeping an eye on Dad through the screen door. He's standing in the phone booth next to the Coca-Cola sign, talking and waving his hands. We can't hear what he's saying because the door's closed and the rain's coming down.

Donny is turning the comics rack around and around, looking at all the choices. There's Archie and Jughead, and Batman and Superman, and comics made from old stories like The Count of

Monte Cristo. Finally Donny picks Mandrake the Magician and takes it to the counter and lays it next to Mom's elbow.

Rita's looking at all the jawbreakers and gum balls. She's trying to figure out how she can get the most for her nickel. Mom says we each get a nickel and that's all. After a while Rita chooses two red gumballs and one Double Bubble gum package. I'm glad she picked Double Bubble because I like reading the Joe Palooka cartoon. Sometimes I don't get them, but I like them anyway.

I'm looking in the freezer box at the popsicles and creamsicles. There's Revels too, and fudgesicles. I can't make up my mind. One minute I decide I want a grape popsicle, then I want a Revel. I pick one up and then I put it back and then I pick up the other.

The Chinese man is standing beside me now with his hand on the glass lid. He's going to shut it, so I'd better decide quick. I grab a grape popsicle.

Finally Mom sees that Dad's hanging up the phone, so she turns and looks around the store, pulls a can of spaghetti sauce down from the shelf and puts it on the counter next to my popsicle and Donny's comic book and Rita's gum. Mom pays the Chinese lady and we go out.

"Did you get the answer to your question?" Mom asks Dad as we walk to the car.

"He just said that Jesus is coming soon, any day now. I asked him if he knew when, and all he said was, 'Very soon.'"

"But what if He's already here? Did you ever think of that?"

Dad stops and looks at Mom as we climb into the car. "What do you mean, 'already here'?"

Mom shrugs and gestures at the whole town and the lake. "Everywhere. Whenever you think about Him, or pray to Him, He's there. That's what they say at St. Andrew's."

Dad looks down at his shoes, then walks around and gets behind the wheel. When Mom slides in beside him he says, "Well, that's not what Pastor Divine says, but even so, I think you're onto something there, Marge." He starts the car.

We're all feeling great. I'm licking my popsicle. Grape, the best flavor of all! Rita blows a bubble and makes it pop. Donny is on the third page of his new book. Shelly keeps taking out the red sucker, looking at the candy on the little round stick, then putting it back in her mouth.

We drive back to the cabin. But then it rains all afternoon and we never get to go back to the beach. Instead we stay inside and play Hearts.

❧❧❧

Now it's Thursday, and I'm afraid that if the rain keeps on falling, I'll never finish my sand castle. It rains on and off all morning, but in the afternoon the sun finally comes out.

My sand castle's a wreck. Just the four corners are left. All the rest is flattened out and washed away. I'll have to build the walls again before I can put in the moats and canals. I hope it doesn't start raining again.

Donny's already swum out more than half way to the buoy line before he has to turn around. Rita has learned to float so she likes to lie on her back in the water with her eyes closed and drift around.

I pat down the walls on my castle again, making sure they're firm. By the end of the afternoon I've got all the walls rebuilt, and then I start bringing over pails of water to fill the moat. I'm just about to start building up the inside part when the rain starts again.

"Donny! Rita! Come in, it's time for supper!" Mom calls. Then she picks up her blankets and bags and yells over to me, "Glenny, time to go! You can finish that tomorrow!" I follow her down to the shore with one of the bags while she waits at the edge for Rita and Donny to swim back. The rain is heavier now and you can see all those little circles where the drops hit the lake. It feels chilly, too.

Mom's holding Shelley's hand while she watches the rain fall. Shelley can talk a little now, but she hardly ever says anything. This time she says something that makes us all laugh. Scowling up at the rain, she yells, "Stupid water!"

❧❧❧

On Friday the clouds are gone and the weather is as fine as the day we got here. We go to the beach early and stay all day. For lunch Mom brings out sandwiches from her cooler, and we wolf them down while standing around her and then we go back to what we were doing.

"Wait, Donny! Don't go swimming right after you've eaten!" She makes him wait a while, so he comes over looking kind of grumpy and stares at the castle I'm building, and pokes his big toe into one of the corner towers.

"Rain's just gonna wash it all away, you know," he tells me. "Two days from now it'll be gone. What's the point?"

I shrug. "This is just the start. You wait! This is going to be the biggest sand castle, ever!" This morning some other kids came over and took a look. "Hey, kid! Pretty neat!" they yelled out to me before they left. Donny shrugs and walks back to the edge of the lake and stands there looking so sad, Mom gets up and puts her hand on his shoulder.

"Donny, you can go in as long as you stay near the edge for another half hour. O.K.?"

"Great!" he says, and dives in.

"Don't go far!" Mom yells. He's already halfway out.

❧❧❧

After dinner and some more games of Hearts, I lie down on my top bunk and stare up at the patterns on the rafters. I can hardly sleep, because I'm so excited about tomorrow. I keep thinking about those turrets and walls and the water in the moats of my finished castle. I'll be sitting at the centre. It'll be the neatest thing I've ever made.

"Glenn, you awake?" Donny whispers. "Don't tell Mom, okay? Tomorrow I'm gonna swim all the way out to the buoys and back."

"Be careful! Mom's scared you might drown!"

"Ah, I won't drown. Don't be stupid."

I don't like it when he calls me stupid. I don't say anything.

It's a very quiet night and I can still hear the wood in the stove burning. Every so often there's a sharp crack when some sparks jump. When I look over the edge of my bunk at Mom and Dad, I see them lying together under their blankets on their bed with the faint glow from the pieces of wood left in the stove. They look

116

peaceful and asleep. Crickets chirp and the wind rushes through the eaves above me. Everything seems just perfect. "Goodnight, Donny," I whisper.

"Goodnight, stupid."

ᥱᢙᥱᢙᥱᢙ

In the middle of the night I wake up because I have to go to the bathroom. I crawl down from the top bunk carefully, trying not to wake up Donny. To get to the outhouse I have to slip out the back door as quietly as possible. The moonlight is bright and I find my way easily. Everything was so perfect when I went to sleep. I don't want to spoil it by waking anybody up. I'm hoping that everything will be just the same in the morning as it was last night.

But when I get back inside the cabin, I see there's somebody sitting up in the main room, in the dark, with a blanket wound around him. It's Dad. He's looking out the window. He seems far away. His eyes glint in the moonlight, but he hardly moves when I come back inside.

"What's the matter, Dad?" I whisper.

He turns from the window. He seems very sad. "I'll tell you in the morning, Glenn. I've had a terrible dream. I think it was a vision. I can't talk about it right now. You just go back to sleep."

I feel pierced by a shaft of anger. But I don't dare say anything, because I don't want to wake anybody up. I turn away and sneak back into my bunk. I pray to Jesus that whatever my Dad saw, it was only a dream.

ᥱᢙᥱᢙᥱᢙ

The next morning's perfect for going to the beach. Mom cooks bacon and eggs and she makes toast by putting bread into a little wire thing she holds over the wood stove. But she doesn't look happy. Neither does Dad. When we're done breakfast he stands up and says, "O.K., listen, everybody. I thought we were going to stay one more day, but the Lord gave me a vision last night. He said we have to go home today."

Mom bangs the dirty pans around in the sink. "A *vision!*"

117

"Look, Marge, I know you're not a strong believer. But when the Lord gives me a vision, I've got to obey it."

Mom dumps a pot of hot water from the wood stove into the sink, puts in some soap and starts scrubbing the pans without answering.

"What did you see?" Donny asks.

"I saw terrible things. I saw the End of Days coming. We've got to get ready."

Donny asks, "When, Dad? When's it going to happen?"

"I'm not sure. Pastor Divine knows. I've got to go talk to him. He'll know what to do."

Donny and I start crying. Rita does, too. Shelley looks confused.

Mom bangs her fry pan around in the sink. "Russell, take a good long look at your children. They love it here! Can't we stay for one more day? That's what was agreed, wasn't it? We were supposed to go away for one week, and it would be a real holiday, and we wouldn't say one word about religion, except for grace at mealtime. Remember?"

Dad looks at all of us, and for a moment it's like he sees us the way he used to, before he met Pastor Divine. He puts his face in his hands, and rubs his eyes, and looks again, and then up at the ceiling, and then he lets out a long sigh.

"I'm sorry. But I've been given a vision, and I just can't ignore it."

Donny lets out a sob. Mom pulls him to her, and then me and Rita too, and suddenly we're all crying into her skirt while she cradles the backs of our heads. Shelley's wailing, too, though she doesn't understand.

Mom looks back at Dad and says, "You just don't get it, do you? He's *already here*! You don't have to do anything. All you've got to do is believe!"

Dad shakes his head slowly. "That's only true during the waiting time. But when the Lord comes on Judgment Day, we've got to be ready. We'll have to do more than believe."

"Fine. Okay, so we'll leave. But when we're back home, if you ever try to make me join Pastor Divine's church, then ...." She doesn't finish.

Dad waits. Finally he asks, "And then, Marge? And then?"

Mom looks down. Softly she finishes, "Then it's over, Russell. Then we're through."

Dad turns around and bangs out the door. As he goes he yells, "Get ready! We're leaving!" He slams the door behind him. I hear the car driving up the street. I bet he's going to the phone booth again.

When we've had enough crying, we load everything back up into the hampers and suitcases and put them on the front porch. By the time Dad comes back we've got most of our stuff packed. We put it in the car and then we get in and he drives up the street so he can give the keys back to the man who rented us the cabin. Donny's gone back to reading his comic book. Over his shoulder I see a picture of a magician in a red cape wiggling his fingers, and in the next picture he's turned into a giant. I wish I could do that. Rita's coloring in her book again and Shelley's asleep. I've borrowed Donny's Superman comic book, but I only read a little bit of it.

When we get onto the highway, for a while we drive down a paved road with tall trees on both sides. Mom's leaning her head against the window, looking away to her right, scowling but not saying anything. I'm sad too, but after a while I forget about that and just watch the trees go by. I like the way all the pine trees are so close together and how they almost crowd right out onto the road. It feels like we're driving through a tunnel toward some dark and mysterious place. When we finally get back into the sunlight, we'll be somewhere totally new.

After a while I stop looking at the trees and notice something else that's really neat. The road we're driving on is hilly, and right in front of us, at the top of the next small hill, it looks like there's a big puddle of water. It looks cool and inviting. As soon as we get close, though, it dries up and then reappears at the top of the next small hill. All the way to Wetaskiwin, I watch the puddles dry up and reappear.

Once we get onto the flat main road to Calgary, the puddles stop. I look over at Dad, who's hunched over the wheel. I'll bet he's still thinking about that terrible vision, turning it over and over in his mind. In the sky ahead of us there's a long, white contrail from a jet plane. Dad glances up at it and then looks back at the road. Donny sees it, too. "We must be close to the air force base!"

Mom's still looking at all farms going by. I know she's wishing she could live in a place like that, all warm and comfy and safe. She grew up on a small farm in Yorkshire, and she often tells us about it. I wish I could go live with her in a place like that. I'd live with her here below, and let Dad and Donny fly away from us into the sky, where they so clearly want to go.

THE END

www.ingramcontent.com/pod-product-compliance
Lightning Source LLC
Chambersburg PA
CBHW020647250626
47154CB00008B/2840